encounters

SIX ONE-ACT PLAYS

leonard melfi

SAMUEL FRENCH, INC.
25 West 45th Street   NEW YORK 10036
7623 Sunset Boulevard   HOLLYWOOD 90046
LONDON   *TORONTO*

For my father and mother

Leonard and Louise Melfi

Contents

Introduction

Off-Off-Broadway had to happen because nothing else was happening. The new anxious American playwrights had no audience to write for; they had no backers to turn to; there was no place to go. You had to be a European (an impossible requirement that was deeply perplexing to a young American playwright) with an established hit somewhere across the ocean—any ocean and in any country other than our country—in order to have your play presented on Broadway, and even Off-Broadway.

It was a terribly frustrating, almost terrifying atmosphere for an American playwright. Thus, coffeehouse theatres, theatres in churches, over hardware stores, in lofts and cellars and garages, began to emerge in various places in Manhattan: Off-Off-Broadway. The miracle drug has become Off-Off-Broadway, but the weary patient is still that same old dying invalid: the commercial, expense-account, scared-stiff-of-the-new-brand-of-playwrighting guys, Broadway theatre. I do believe, however, most sincerely, and with much hope, that Off-Off-Broadway will revive Off-Broadway once again, and perhaps even eventually influence *Broadway*. I am also quite certain that Miss Ellen Stewart happens once in a lifetime, and I am so very glad that it was during my lifetime.

Ellen Stewart is *LaMama*, and by now, anyone who knows anything at all about the contemporary American theatre is well aware of who and what LaMama is. She has unselfishly committed herself to bringing to life the plays of the new American playwrights. She wants nothing in return but to see us go forward, to be sure that our stomachs are full, to make certain that we are always encouraged . . . and that we continue to write our plays. Sometimes she designs dresses—beautiful, chic, and very feminine dresses—for seven days a week in order to be able to afford the pressing weekly expenses of running Café LaMama; all we have to do is write our plays.

I came to New York City from Binghamton, N.Y., via a two-year stay in Europe, just about eight years ago. I wanted to be an actor and enrolled in an acting school. After a couple of very uncertain years, I decided that I would much rather write plays.

I wrote four full-length plays before I wrote my first one-act play. I don't know where the copies of these plays are right now and I like it better that way. Four extra-long *autobiographical* works for the stage before I was even twenty-five!

During the late summer of 1962 I wrote my first one-act play. I was walking up my street, East Ninth Street, when I discovered for the first time a basement coffeehouse which was also a theatre doing one-act plays by new untried playwrights. A bright, hand-painted sign hung up over the basement window at street level; it spelled out boldly: "Café LaMama Presents." I met Paul Foster, another beginning playwright, there. He was part of the very start of the coffeehouse theatre in that low basement on East Ninth Street, and was then acting more or less as a barker. He was standing out on the sidewalk to get people who passed by to come down and see the show—that day I was one of the people. I was impressed by the play, and after it was over I went home thinking more seriously than ever before about being a playwright. In a few days' time I was sitting down at my typewriter. I soon met Paul again in front of that basement coffeehouse theatre, and I gave him the two plays

I had finished. He liked them both and passed them on to Ellen Stewart, who decided to produce the one called *Lazy Baby Susan*. It was also the first time that I met Ellen Stewart, *LaMama herself!* Her coffeehouse theatre was a long narrow basement which seated about twenty-five people at the most. During the rehearsals of *Lazy Baby Susan*, which opened on October 26, 1962, directed by Gino Ardito, Ellen had a wall torn down so that LaMama could at least seat forty people. I was earning a living then as a semi-carpenter and part-time refinisher of furniture, and so I built some extra tables for her. (I am very pleased that she still uses those same simple tables at Café LaMama, which has since moved twice, and is now located at 122 Second Avenue.)

Lazy Baby Susan was a "big smash hit" all thirty minutes of it. And then I did a pretty stupid thing: I went back to "peddling" the four extra-long, full-length autobiographical plays for Broadway. I got nowhere. In the naïve process, I half-disregarded LaMama. But no matter, there was always Ellen Stewart in the neighborhood. We'd bump into each other quite often; she'd smile and give me a look with those knowing eyes of hers; and there suddenly would seem to be instant encouragement in the Lower East Side air. Ellen was aware that I should have continued with my one-acters, and I was too, but I was stubborn. I suppose at the time I didn't have the sort of faith that Ellen had.

Then in the summer of 1964 Theatre Genesis was formed by a very sincere and serious director, Ralph Cook, at St. Mark's Church in-the-Bowery. Each Monday night, sessions were held in the modest upstairs theatre in the back of the church. The Monday night meetings were for the sole purpose of having new plays read for the first time, an idea and practice that I will always believe to be invaluable for the playwright, any playwright. My first two one-act plays "flopped" in their Monday night readings at Theatre Genesis. I was a bit depressed by it all, but David Miller, an actor, had introduced me to Theatre Genesis, and he continued to "shoot me up" with confidence. And then, of course, there was always Ellen Stewart and our impromptu meetings on the corners and the streets of the East Village neighborhood: more extra enlightenment.

I sat down and wrote another one-act play, *Coffeecake and Caviar*. I had been watching a certain actor at Theatre Genesis on Monday nights, Kevin O'Connor, and I thought that he was the best around. I gave him a copy of *Coffeecake and Caviar* to read. He, in turn, "found" Barbara Young for me, for the girl's part. They both read it on a Monday night and it went over beautifully. Ralph Cook decided to do it at Theatre Genesis along with another one-act play of mine called *Sunglasses*, with another fine actress, Stephanie Gordon. It was then that *Coffeecake and Caviar* became *Birdbath*, and it opened at Theatre Genesis for three weeks on June 11, 1965. Ellen Stewart came over to see it and afterward immediately decided to send it to Europe on a LaMama tour; hence, LaMama gave the play its original European productions in Paris and Copenhagen. It was then produced here again in America, first at La-Mama and then as part of the bill, *Six From LaMama*, Off-Broadway, at the Martinique Theatre, produced by Theodore Mann and Paul Libin, under the Circle-in-the-Square banner and directed by the imaginative Tom O'Horgan, who also directed it in Europe. It opened at the Martinique on April 11, 1966. (A month later, Mari-Claire Charba received an Obie, an Off-Broadway award, for her performance as Velma Sparrow.)

During the two-year period since my introduction to Theatre Genesis, I have written over twenty one-act plays, nearly all of which were given readings at Theatre Genesis, and six one-act plays, five of which were produced at Theatre Genesis, and the other at LaMama.

Birdbath was written during a time when I was almost always dealing with people who were practically strangers to me, but whose lives and beings suddenly seemed more meaningful than my own existence. (The excellent production of *Birdbath,* presented one afternoon at the Actors Studio, was due to the direction of Arthur Storch.)

Lunchtime was meant to be funny and was also based on my own experiences as a furniture refinisher. But it turned out to be more of a small tragicomedy.

Halloween played for five nights, beginning on October 27, 1966, at The Playwrights' Unit sponsored by Albee-Barr-and-Wilder. Then, like *Birdbath,* it was also done at the Actors Studio.

Ferryboat was produced at Theatre Genesis, where it opened on September 2, 1965, as a curtain-raiser to another one-act play of mine: it became the more successful one of the two on the double bill. Like the other plays in this collection, it was another encounter, and since the ride on the Staten Island Ferry is one of my truly favorite pastimes, it was only inevitable that I write *Ferryboat.*

The Shirt was first read at Theatre Genesis, and then in July of 1966 it was given a staged reading at The Eugene O'Neill Memorial Theatre Foundation in Waterford, Connecticut, where I was invited to be a playwright-in-residence. Like *Halloween,* it was directed by Melvin Bernhardt.

Times Square was performed by the LaMama troupe under Tom O'Horgan's direction at various festivals throughout Europe this past summer. It premiered in Frankfurt, and then went on to the Netherlands, Milan, Turin, Stockholm, Denmark, Edinburgh, London, Liverpool, and the International Drama Festival in Belgrade.

Kevin O'Connor, who has become an exceptional friend, acted in all of my plays produced Off-Off-Broadway because he is an exceptional actor as well. I mention this because some of the finest actors are coming out of Off-Off-Broadway, and also because I will always be grateful to good actors and actresses (Stephanie Gordon, Barbara

Young, Mari-Claire Charba); their importance will never be taken for granted as long as I write plays.

I am absolutely thankful for all of these people, and others too numerous to mention. I am especially grateful to a dear friend, Elaine Dundy, whose interest in caring for my work has been undying.

If Off-Off-Broadway did not happen I would still be trying to peddle the first four full-length plays. If Off-Off-Broadway did not happen I believe that I would never have written the twenty or more one-act plays. I believe, also, that I may never have gone on to writing my new full-length plays.

However, things were not always that smooth, especially for LaMama. There were always financial problems (there still are), there were the problems with Actors Equity who demanded salaries for the actors, and in November of 1965 LaMama had one week left to meet the safety requirements of the Fire Department. Thirty LaMama playwrights got together and each came up with a three-minute play for a special week-long benefit. Everyone volunteered their services—actors, directors, technicians—and we came out with a show called *Bang!* The money was raised and so were all our spirits. After long but finally successful sessions with Equity, the union agreed that Café LaMama could continue without paying Equity actors as long as no admission was charged for performances.

What is taking place now, and has been taking place for a number of years, in the cellars and the lofts of New York City, is the most important thing that has yet happened to the American Theatre. There are no pressures. One can explore with an audience, make mistakes before an audience, correct those mistakes for an audience. There is less need to worry and more need to perfect, to experiment. That is the key word . . . experiment . . . to look ahead toward the *new*.

Leonard Melfi

Birdbath

BIRDBATH *was first presented by Theatre Genesis on June 11, 1965, at St. Mark's Church in-the-Bowery, New York City, with the following cast:*

(*In order of appearance*)

FRANKIE BASTA   Kevin O'Connor
VELMA SPARROW   Barbara Young

Directed by Ralph Cook

Subsequently, BIRDBATH *was presented by Theodore Mann and Paul Libin with the Circle-in-the-Square on April 11, 1966, at the Martinique Theatre, New York City, as part of the bill,* Six From LaMama, *with the following cast:*

(*In order of appearance*)

FRANKIE BASTA   Kevin O'Connor
VELMA SPARROW   Mari-Claire Charba

Directed by Tom O'Horgan

THE PEOPLE OF THE PLAY

FRANKIE BASTA,   a poet in his late 20's.

VELMA SPARROW,   26, a nervous and troubled young lady who is a rapid speaker and sometimes trembles.

WHERE THEY ARE

New York City: a midtown cafeteria, the streets outside, and FRANKIE's basement apartment.

WHEN

Contemporary: a night in February. The action is con-
tinuous.

Hazy music coming from a piped-in system. The curtain rises. We are in a garishly lit cafeteria. To our right we see FRANKIE BASTA *behind the cash booth before the cash register. He lights a cigarette, eyes his wrist watch, and then begins to read a book.*

To our left we see VELMA SPARROW. *She is clearing off a table in her working area. As she wipes the surface we are aware of her delicate, slow and easy nature, fused together with strange anxiety. Every so often she gives a quick look over at* FRANKIE. *He, in turn, does the same thing. But their eyes never meet. They never catch each other. It is almost as though they both know the precise moment when to steal their brief glances without being noticed. This little "game of glances" goes on for about two minutes before they are finally caught staring at each other, both face-to-face. There is a pause wherein they both seem semi-mesmerized, as they both continue to stare at each other.*

FRANKIE Hi.

VELMA Hi.

FRANKIE How are you doing?

VELMA (*Shrugging*) Okay . . . I guess.
(*She goes back to her work;* FRANKIE *goes back to his book*)

VELMA (*Going over to him*) What's your name?

FRANKIE (*Looking up*) Frankie. What's yours?

VELMA　Velma

FRANKIE　I'm glad to meet you, Velma.

VELMA　Likewise, I'm sure. (FRANKIE *smiles*) You jist started workin' here tonight, didn't you?

FRANKIE　Yeah. That's right.

VELMA　And you don't like it, do you?

FRANKIE　How can you tell that?

VELMA　By the way you look.

FRANKIE　How's that?

VELMA　Well, first of all, if you don't mind my sayin' so, you jist don't look like you belong in a lousy place like this. I think you look pretty high-class to me. My mother would really go for you.

FRANKIE　Yeah? How old is your old lady—I mean your mother?

VELMA　(*Giggling*)　Oh, I didn't mean that way, Frankie! Now you got me blushin'. My face is red, huh? If my mother was here she'd really be blushin'. What I meant to say was she'd think you were jist *right* . . .

FRANKIE　Right for what?

VELMA　I . . . I . . . oh, I don't know how to say it. Forget it . . . I guess. But do you know what, Frankie?

FRANKIE　(*Kindly*)　What's that, Velma?

VELMA　Well, I used to be real skinny, you know what I mean? I used to be all bones, almost like one of them skeletons. But since I been workin' here for Mr. Quincy, well, I've been puttin' on some weight. (*She pauses*)

That's why, in a way, this job isn't really that bad—because of the free meal they let you have. My mother said to me, "Velma, you take advantage of that free meal. You eat as much as you can . . . when something's free you make use of it . . . take as much as they let you have." And so, I've been eating pretty good lately, and Mr. Quincy, he's a nice man, he never tells me that I'm eating too much. In fact, I think he's a real nice man, because he hired me without my having any experience at all. This is the first time I've ever had a job where I cleaned off the tables and everything when the people were through eating. Boy, at first I was real scared about this job. I didn't think I was gonna be able to do it right . . . you know?

FRANKIE   You're doing okay . . .

VELMA   Although, you know what?
(*She starts to bite her fingernails*)

FRANKIE   What's that, Velma?

VELMA   Well, sometimes Mr. Quincy says things to me . . . or he gives me certain kinds of looks . . . like for instance . . . (*Embarrassed*) I was his . . . *girl friend,* maybe. (*She looks at* FRANKIE, *waiting hopefully for him to agree with her.* FRANKIE *gives her a slight smile of comfort, but it is not a smile of agreement*) I told my mother about the way Mr. Quincy is to me sometimes, and right away she wanted to come down and meet him. She asked me how old he was and she wanted to know how he looked, and after I told her everything she wanted to know, she said that some night she would get all dressed up and then come down here and wait for me until I got off, and while she was waiting I could introduce her to Mr. Quincy. (*She walks away and begins to wipe the same table top over again*) You know what she said to me, my mother? She said that it was all up in my mind that Mr. Quincy might jist be . . . *interested* . . . in me. She said that it wasn't true and that I should jist concentrate on my job and forget about all those pipe dreams, otherwise I would be gettin' fired. (*She pauses*) Sometimes . . . sometimes it's so hard for me to figure my mother out . . . because right afterwards she's tellin' me that maybe I shouldn't eat so much after all because then I would be goin' from one extreme to the other. She said when I was real skinny I couldn't find a nice boy, and, well, if I kept on eating the way I've been doing lately I'd get real fat, and so it would still be the same old story for me. (*She laughs a desperate, frantic sort of laugh*) My mother . . . changes her mind so much sometimes . . . that it gives me a headache.

(*She begins to wipe the table top with great pressure.* FRANKIE *watches her for a moment*)

FRANKIE (*Lightly*) Velma, what are you trying to do?

VELMA (*Quickly*) What?

FRANKIE Are you trying to wear that table top off?

VELMA Oh . . . yes . . . I know what you mean.

FRANKIE You can get a headache just by doing things like that, Velma.

VELMA Yeah . . . I guess you're right. (*She goes back over to him*) You know something?

FRANKIE Yes? I'm listening to you, Velma.

VELMA Oh, what a funny coincidence. That's what I was jist goin' to say to you, Frankie. I was goin' to say: you know something? You make me feel good, Frankie, because you're listening to me. And then I was goin' to thank you for it, and tell you how much I appreciated our conversation with each other. There's not too many people I can talk to. Or what I should say is that there's not too many people who will listen to me because they think I talk too much. (FRANKIE *glances at his wrist watch*) It's almost time to go, huh?

FRANKIE   Five minutes and we'll be free.

VELMA   You really don't like this job, I can tell. You can't wait to get out of here, can you?

FRANKIE   You know what you're talking about.

VELMA   But I don't know as much as you.

FRANKIE   You can't really say things like that.

VELMA (*After a pause*)   What . . . do you do . . . when you leave here? I mean, if you don't mind my askin'. I know it's none of my business . . .

FRANKIE   I would like to go out and get drunk!

VELMA   Boy, do you sound mad all of a sudden.

FRANKIE   That's the way I am sometimes.

VELMA (*Rapidly*)   Are you married?

FRANKIE (*Trying to be pleasant*)   Velma . . . I have a hard time just taking care of myself.

VELMA (*After a pause*)   You know, you really look nice. You don't belong here, that's all there is to it. You should be in the movies. You know what I mean? You could be an actor. I always wanted to be in the movies. I'd love to be an actress, but my mother says I'm not pretty enough . . . and I guess she's right . . . or was she?

FRANKIE   Why don't you relax, Velma?

VELMA   How come you're telling me that?

FRANKIE   You're shaking. You should learn how to be calm. It would make things a lot easier for you.

VELMA   (*Very nervously*) Well, it's almost time, isn't it? It's almost midnight . . . time to quit and everything . . . so I better go and change. (*She starts to move away, but it is an immense effort for her to do so*) I'll see you again tomorrow night, Frankie, okay?

FRANKIE   Sure . . . okay . . . Velma.

VELMA   (*Running off*) 'Bye! And nice talkin' to you . . . (*She is gone*)

FRANKIE   'Bye . . . (*Then, more to himself*) Nice talkin' to you, too.
  (*A quick blackout. The lights come up again. We are on the streets outside.* VELMA *is standing alone. She is out of breath. Then* FRANKIE *enters from our right*)

VELMA   Hi, Frankie.

FRANKIE   What are you doing here?

VELMA   I . . . I . . . left . . . before you did! I've been standin' here waitin' for you!

FRANKIE   You're shivering to death.

VELMA   I was jist wonderin' if you would walk me to the subway. I'm usually never afraid, but tonight, well, I jist can't explain why I got the jitters.

FRANKIE   Where do you live?

VELMA   In the Bronx. It's pretty far. It takes about an hour on the subway. Where do you live?

FRANKIE   Around the corner.

VELMA   Oh, geez! You're lucky! I wish I lived near where I worked. My other job is jist as far away as this one. I never have any luck when it comes to my jobs.

FRANKIE   You mean you have another job?

VELMA   My mother wants me to. She says we need the money. For a while I only had the day job. But my mother said it wasn't enough. So then I got this job from Mr. Quincy about a month ago. He's a real nice man. I'll bet if you get to know him he'd be a lot like the way my father was.

FRANKIE   Your father dead?

VELMA   We really don't know. He might be. I ain't seen him since I was six years old. That's twenty years ago. I'm twenty-six.

FRANKIE   What did he do? Where did he go?

VELMA   He deserted us and no one's been able to find him since. But actually, he didn't leave me and my brother Herbert; it was my mother who he left. He said that if he didn't run away my mother would drive him nuts. But I don't think that would'uve happened because she didn't drive me and my brother Herbert nuts. We're both okay. Of course Herbert hasn't lived with us for a long time now. He got married when he was only nineteen and we hardly ever see him any more. Do you know something? You're almost as handsome as Herbert. He's the most handsome person you ever saw. My mother always wanted him to be a movie star, and he could'uve been too if he didn't run away and get married like he did. My mother never stopped telling him that he was going to make a lot of money someday for all of us and that we would be so proud of him because he would be famous throughout the whole world. (*Very wistfully*) I wish he would'uve listened to her. Then I wouldn't have to work any more.

FRANKIE   It's getting pretty cold standing here, Velma. One thing I don't like is cold weather. Let's start walking toward the subway.

VELMA   Okay.
         (*They begin to walk*)

FRANKIE   Wouldn't you know that I would be born during the month that has the lousiest weather?

VELMA   (*After giving a long sigh*)   We should celebrate, Frankie!

FRANKIE   Why?

VELMA   I was born in February, too.

FRANKIE   Congratulations.

VELMA   Ain't that a coincidence?

FRANKIE   Sure is. And it's also getting colder.

VELMA   When is yours?

FRANKIE   When is my what?

VELMA   The date. Mine's already gone. It was the seventh.

FRANKIE   Well, happy birthday anyway, Velma. Mine hasn't arrived yet. It's the twenty-first.

VELMA   Well, then, when I see you on the twenty-first, I'll wish you yours, too.

FRANKIE   You do that.

VELMA   You jist sound so unhappy compared to when we first started talking tonight. February isn't that bad a month. I think it's the *best* month of all, Frankie.

FRANKIE   How do you figure that?

VELMA   Because of the people born in this month. There's George Washington, and Abraham Lincoln . . . and there's . . . *tomorrow!*

FRANKIE   What's tomorrow?

VELMA   Saint Valentine's Day!

FRANKIE   Oh . . . yeah . . .

VELMA   You won't believe this . . . but . . . I never once got a valentine in my whole life.

FRANKIE (*After a long pause, uneasily*)   It's getting colder by the minute, isn't it, Velma?

VELMA   But do you know, Frankie, I didn't mind too much. My mother used to take me to Schrafft's and then afterwards we'd go to the Radio City Music Hall every Valentine's Day while I was still going to school. She said it would take my mind off not getting any valentines. My mother did good things for me except sometimes she would yell at me and say that I was homely and skinny and that I shook too much and it made her nervous and so she'd scream at me to go into another room so's she wouldn't have to look at me for a while . . .

FRANKIE (*Quickly*)   This is it! You want to come in for a minute?
    (*He stops and so does* VELMA)

VELMA   Come in where, Frankie?

FRANKIE   This is where I live. Do you want to come in for
some coffee? It'll warm you up.

VELMA   I really got to get back home. My mother will be
waitin' up for me . . . and . . . oh . . .

FRANKIE   C'mon. Look, you're trembling because it's cold
out here. It's even beginning to snow now.

VELMA   No, no. I'm not trembling because I'm cold. You
know now how I tremble a lot, don't you? I'm really
warm. I almost feel as though I'm beginnin' to sweat, as
though it was the summertime, or because I was worried
about something.

FRANKIE   What are you worried about, then?

VELMA   Well, I started to say before that my mother would
be . . . waitin' up for me . . . but . . .

FRANKIE   All right, then. C'mon, I'll walk you to your subway. I can't waste any more goddam time!

VELMA   No, Frankie! I forgot! You see . . . my mother's
not home . . . I mean, she *is* home but she's not waitin'
up for me tonight . . . and so . . .

FRANKIE   Yes? So?

VELMA   So I suppose it'll be all right if I come in for a few
minutes. I guess I really would enjoy some hot coffee before I leave . . . for home.
    (FRANKIE *takes out his keys and walks down the
    steps to his apartment. He opens the door and turns
    on the light*)

FRANKIE   Well? Are you coming in, Velma?
    (VELMA *is trembling almost violently*)

VELMA   (*Standing on the stairs*)   I . . . I . . . yes . . .
I'm coming . . .

FRANKIE   Jesus! Control yourself, will you?

VELMA   I'll be okay, Frankie, in a minute. It's jist that I've never been in a man's apartment before. It's jist that I've never been alone with a man before. Oh, I forgot . . .

FRANKIE   Hey! I don't have much patience left, Velma!

VELMA   I forgot that I *was* alone with a man before. My brother Herbert. But that doesn't really count, does it? Because he's my brother, huh, Frankie?

FRANKIE   If you don't come down here in one more second, I'm shutting the door on you and you're walking to the subway by yourself!

VELMA   (*Finally going down the stairs*) You know, Frankie, maybe instead of the coffee I'd better have hot tea instead. (*The lights are beginning to dim*) My mother says . . . she *used* to say . . . that I drank too much coffee. Ever since I was a little girl I drank coffee, and she always told me that that was why I was so skinny and not very tall like most girls, and that's why I shake so much, and that's why I'll probably never find a nice man to marry me someday . . . but now I'm gaining weight and everything . . .
    (*Complete blackout. We hear music now. It is the old-time, dance-band type of music coming from a phonograph. The lights slowly come back up. We are in* FRANKIE's *apartment.* VELMA *is sitting on the edge of the bed drinking her hot tea.* FRANKIE *is standing up before the refrigerator with the door opened; he is drinking from a bottle*)

VELMA   I don't wanna sound stupid or anything, Frankie, but what's the name of that record?
    (FRANKIE *takes another long slug, puts the bottle back into the refrigerator and slams the door shut*)

FRANKIE (*Turning around, facing* VELMA *with a smile*) "I Only Have Eyes for You."
> (VELMA *blushes and turns her face away; she stifles a giggle*)

VELMA   It's a pretty song . . .

FRANKIE (*With half-a-sigh*)   It sure is! Makes me nostalgic. That's why I'm playing it, because I like feeling nostalgic . . .

VELMA   I don't know what it means . . .

FRANKIE   They used to play this song when I was in high school. It was the theme song of the ole' hometown band.

VELMA   I'll bet you had as much girls chasin' you as my brother Herbert did.

FRANKIE (*Singing*)   "Are the stars out tonight? . . . I don't know if it's cloudy or bright . . ."

VELMA (*Embarrassed*)   It's certainly a romantic song. (*She sips her tea*)

FRANKIE   ". . . 'cause I only have eyes for you . . ." (*He begins to dance*) Would you like to dance with me, Velma?
> (*He bows to her*)

VELMA (*Really embarrassed*)   Oh . . . I . . . I forgot to tell you. But I *did* get a few valentines when I was younger. My brother Herbert used to mail them to me.

FRANKIE   Jesus Christ! Will you shut the hell up about your goddam brother Herbert!

VELMA   Geez . . . you get mad easy, don't you?

FRANKIE   And stop trembling like that. My bed's going to fall apart.

(*He goes back to the refrigerator and takes out the bottle*)

VELMA   You drink a lot, too, don't you?

FRANKIE (*Drinking*)   No shit, baby!

VELMA   And . . . when you drink . . . you curse a lot, too, don't you?

FRANKIE   You don't like it?

VELMA   No . . .

FRANKIE (*Pausing, then smiling*)   I'm sorry . . . Velma.

VELMA   What's that you're drinkin'? If you don't mind my askin'?

FRANKIE   Ice-cold martinis. Already mixed. You can buy it in any liquor store, all prepared, ready and waiting for you. Saves lots of time, you know. Not too much time left . . . Velma . . . Sparrow!

VELMA   How . . . did you know my last name? I never told it to you.

FRANKIE   I guessed.

VELMA   Aw, c'mon, I don't believe you.

FRANKIE   Honest to God, I did.

VELMA   It's spooky then, don't you think?

FRANKIE   Not at all. It's a beautiful name, Velma. It goes perfect with you.

VELMA   I didn't tell it to you before because I've always been ashamed of it.

FRANKIE   How could you be?

VELMA When I was in school the kids used to always whisper behind my back. They'd say: here she comes, here comes Velma the ugly sparrow.

FRANKIE You forget about those creeps!

VELMA Well, you know what I did? I quit school jist so's I wouldn't have to listen to them any more. And I only had a year left before I would'uve got my diploma, too. Sometimes I think about going to night school, but my mother says it's all too late now. You know, my mother is a peculiar woman. First she's sayin' to me, "Velma, we gotta save money, that's all there is to it!" And then . . . the very next minute she's askin' me to loan her five dollars for the beauty parlor or something like that.

FRANKIE Doesn't your mother work?

VELMA You sound mad again.

FRANKIE I am mad again!
        (*He takes another swig of the bottle*)

VELMA No, she doesn't work because she usually doesn't feel too well. That's why I have two jobs. During the days I work in a movie house in Greenwich Village. I'm an usherette. My mother didn't want me to work down there at first because she thinks the Village is dangerous. She doesn't like the idea of me being around all those fairies and those leprechauns. Well, I'm not afraid of the fairies but *those leprechauns* really scare me.

FRANKIE (*Scratching his head*) What do you mean by leprechauns?

VELMA You know what I mean: those girls who don't like men; they like to be with women instead.

FRANKIE Uh, Lesbians, Velma, Lesbians. Not leprechauns.

VELMA Oh, that's right, Les—bi—ans.
(FRANKIE *takes off his shoes and socks*)

FRANKIE I'm making myself comfortable, so don't worry about a thing.

VELMA Oh, well, it's your apartment, so why should I mind, huh? Besides, I don't really mind anything right now. I'm having a good time here with you. (*She looks around*) This is a real artist's apartment, isn't it?

FRANKIE If you think so.

VELMA So Frankie, what do you do? I know that being a cashier isn't your life. You're too handsome for that. And you're too smart. I've never seen so many books in all my life.

FRANKIE I'm a writer, Velma.

VELMA (*Thrilled*) Gee! You must have a big imagination! You'll probably be rich and famous some day, and then I'll be able to say that I knew you, won't I?

FRANKIE I'm a poet, really. Poets don't make very much money, and they hardly ever become famous.

VELMA Who's that on the wall? He looks real familiar to me.

FRANKIE That's Van Gogh. A self-portrait.

VELMA (*Excited*) Did he give it to you?

FRANKIE No, Velma.

VELMA And who are these people in this picture? (*She looks closer*) Oh! You're in the picture, too! It must be your family, huh?

FRANKIE That's right.

VELMA   They all look so happy: your father and mother and sister and brother . . . and you! Are they all happy as the picture?

FRANKIE   Yes, they are, most of the time. I'm pretty proud of them . . . and they're pretty patient with me.

VELMA   You're soooooo . . . lucky!

FRANKIE   Why's that?

VELMA   To be able to have such a nice family.
      (FRANKIE *drinks some more*)

FRANKIE   I'm getting stoned . . . drunk, Velma. Don't mind me if I do. I might get a little vulgar . . . a little truthful . . . I might start talking about myself . . . but I'll try to be nice . . . I really . . . *like you,* Velma!

VELMA (*Nervously*)   And do you know who else was born during this month? My favorite actress! And you probably like her because she is the most beautiful woman in the entire world!

FRANKIE   Who's that?

VELMA   Elizabeth Taylor! What do you think of that?

FRANKIE   Liz, huh? Marvelous! We're in good company, aren't we, Velma?

VELMA   I knew you'd like to hear that.

FRANKIE   Velma, I'm going to make myself some tea. I really shouldn't be getting this drunk. I'm a bad host, huh?

VELMA   Oh, no, I don't think so at all.

FRANKIE   Thank you. You're beautiful.

VELMA   I don't know what . . . to say . . .

FRANKIE   You don't have to say anything. Just keep me company, that's all.

VELMA   I like you when you drink. It's like watching a show on TV or something. You never know what to expect next. First you're very funny and then you're very mad. In a way, it's fun. (*There is a pause*) I'll bet I know why you don't have a TV set here.

FRANKIE (*Trying to make some tea*)   Why?

VELMA   Because if you had a TV set then you wouldn't write your poems, would you?

FRANKIE   You're very much on the ball.

VELMA   I wouldn't know what to do without a TV set in the house. My mother and me, we sit and watch all of the *love* stories! I used to go to Loeee's Paradise a lot. You ever been there?

FRANKIE   What is it?

VELMA   A movie house. It's jist like a castle out of the fairy tales. You really dream there: Loeee's Paradise!

FRANKIE   It's *Loew's* Paradise, not *Loeee's*, isn't it?

VELMA   It is? Geez. My mother and me have always called it *Loeee's*, and we've been goin' there for years and years. But you must be right because you're educated and because you're an artist.

FRANKIE   Where is this place?

VELMA   It's in the Bronx. I used to go on Saturday nights. They have stars on the ceilings. Thousands of stars twinkling on and off. It's like another world. And if you sit right in the middle of the theatre there's a big full moon above your head. It's so romantic. You should see it! But . . . I stopped goin' because most of the girls and the boys go in couples and they all try to sit underneath the big full moon . . . and I was beginning to feel out of place.

FRANKIE Velma, do you want more tea?

VELMA I was thinkin' that maybe I'd like jist a little sip of that martini mix, if you don't care, Frankie?

FRANKIE Of course I don't care. It's my pleasure. (*He pours her a glass*) Salut!

VELMA (*Lifting the glass*) Cheers . . .

FRANKIE Cheers then. It's all the same.
(*He drinks more too*)

VELMA It's strong . . . but I like it.

FRANKIE Very good. Enjoy yourself.

VELMA This is a real treat. I like treats. Every payday when I bring home the money, my mother decided that we both should have a treat, and so the next morning, every single week that I can remember, we have coffee-cake and caviar for breakfast!

FRANKIE Coffeecake and caviar?

VELMA Oh, it's delicious together. Some day you'll have to come to our apartment for breakfast. You'll love it . . .
(*She sips some more*)

FRANKIE Drink up, Velma. There's a lot more yet. Relax.
(FRANKIE *flops down on the bed next to her*) My head is beginning to spin.
(VELMA *immediately rises from the bed*)

VELMA (*Trembling*) I used to work at The Merry-Go-Round Club once. I was the hat-check girl, but my mother said they fired me because they wanted a girl who was prettier than me. Do you know that it was my favorite job, though, even if it didn't last very long. I saw all the stars and the celebrities. Once I even saw Ed Sullivan!

FRANKIE Relax, Velma.

VELMA (*Drinking some more*) Oh, I'm okay. I'm relaxed. (*She goes to his desk*) This is where you write, huh?

FRANKIE When I'm working on my book.

VELMA You're writing a book too? You really are smart! I'll bet you're a good typist, too, aren't you?

FRANKIE I never compose my poetry on the typewriter; only my book.
(VELMA *sits down at his desk*)

VELMA Well . . . anyway . . .
(*She finishes the drink rapidly.* FRANKIE *sits up on his bed and stares over at her*)

FRANKIE You want more?

VELMA I don't think I'd better. I'm gettin' sleepy now. Maybe I'd better go home . . . my mother is . . . well, she's *not!* . . . really . . .

FRANKIE I would like to hug you, Velma. I would like very much to put my arms around you, and I would like to hold you ever so gently, and I would like to whisper tenderly in your ear; I would like to say to you: "Velma-honey, believe me, little-girl-Velma, things are not really that bad. Everything's going to be all right, okay, you just wait and see. Take my word for it, Velma."

(VELMA *does not know what to do; she glances back and forth at her wrist watch*)

VELMA   Well! It's Valentine's Day now! I'll bet you have so many girl friends, don't you? I can jist see it in the morning when you wake up. Your mailbox will be stuffed with hundreds of valentines, won't it? From all your girl friends?

FRANKIE   It used to be that way once, but no more, and I like it that way. You see, Velma, most girls, after they flip their corks over me, find out pretty fast that they don't go for me anymore. They discover that there is competition. They believe I'd rather make it with my typewriter. Did you know that every chick I've ever sacked becomes insanely jealous of that innocent little machine over there on my desk? Isn't that the stupidest thing you ever heard of? Harmless portable! . . . in-animate black mother, old pawnshop object that never gives me any bullshit!

VELMA   You're really somethin'.

FRANKIE   Would you bother me if I sat down and typed away whenever I felt that I had to, whenever the urge was suddenly the most important thing in my life? You'd leave me alone, wouldn't you?

VELMA   Yes . . .

FRANKIE   You wouldn't show any signs of bitterness, would you?

VELMA   No . . .

FRANKIE   (*Drinking some more*)   I knew you wouldn't let me down, Velma. You see, these chicks, almost all of them, they want all of your time and all of your attention. They say they understand you, but when it comes right

down to the actual test, well, their lovely precious pussies panic! And so what do you do? You make it with a guy and there's just as much bullshit there too! (*Quietly*) The thing to do is to find out where the hell the right chick is . . . under my bed? . . . in the bathroom? . . . up in the Bronx, maybe? (VELMA *giggles*, FRANKIE *sips his drink*) I'll tell you something: I'd rather *come* all over the keys of that hot typewriter . . . that's the way I feel sometimes! (*He gets up from the bed*) Besides . . . (*He laughs bitterly*) maybe it's not such a bad idea . . . it's a whole lot safer. No sweat. How can you knock up a typewriter? (*He stops and stares at her*) But . . . you don't even know what I'm talking about, do you? (VELMA *simply smiles back at him*) Anyway, that answers your question about how many valentines I'll be getting in the morning. (*He begins to take off his shirt.* VELMA *gets up*) Don't worry about anything. I'm only making myself comfortable, that's all. (*He takes off his pants*) Will you please sit down? I'm not going to harm you.
> (*He goes into the bathroom*)

VELMA   Please don't get mad at me, Frankie.

FRANKIE (*Offstage*)   I'm not getting mad at you. I'm just disappointed, that's all.
> (*He begins to sing and/or hum his song from the bathroom. Then he returns in a bathrobe*)

VELMA (*After a moment*)   Maybe I can stay here, jist for a little while? My mother won't even know about it . . . since she's not waitin' up for me . . .
> (*She begins to shake again*)

FRANKIE   You're confusing me, baby, and I get confused enough when I got gin in my belly. Make up your mind. And forget about your mother. I'm sick and tired of hearing about your old lady!

VELMA Okay . . .

FRANKIE If I give you just a small glass of this martini mix, it'll make you stop shaking like that. (*He goes and pours her some more*) Now here. Take it and drink it in one gulp.

VELMA Will it? Will it make my shaking stop?

FRANKIE Don't ask questions. Just do as I told you.

VELMA Okay . . .
(*She manages to get it all down in one swig*)

FRANKIE You see? You did it. Now come back over here and sit down like before and make yourself at home. And take your coat back off. (VELMA *walks away from him and sits back down at the desk*) Well, aren't you going to take your coat off?

VELMA In a minute, Frankie, in a minute.

FRANKIE Velma? You want to know something?

VELMA What, Frankie?

FRANKIE I'm glad that you came home with me tonight. You're the first woman I've had here in a long time. (VELMA *shows signs of wanting to leave. She nervously notices a book lying on the desk*)

VELMA (*Reading, as she picks the book up*) "Poet in New York . . ."

FRANKIE A great goddam good poet, too, let me tell you!

VELMA Fed—er—ico . . . Garcia . . . Lorca . . .

FRANKIE And God bless him! Amen.

VELMA I . . . never heard of him. Is he a Puerto Rican?

FRANKIE (*Softly*)   Where did I find you?

VELMA   Does he still live in New York?

FRANKIE   Oh, sure. He's pushing boo up in East Harlem for the winter.

VELMA   Oh.

FRANKIE (*Going to her*)   Please . . . let me just hold you, Velma, okay? (VELMA *shows signs of wanting to leave again*) Don't move! Stay where you are . . . I'm not going to harm you. If only you'll believe that, then everything will be okay. Take my word for it, please . . . okay?
(*He gives her a very honest smile*)

VELMA (*After a moment*)   Okay . . . I guess.

FRANKIE   Good, Velma. Besides, I need someone to talk to, and you need someone to talk to. Right?

VELMA   Right, I guess.

FRANKIE   In other words, we both need someone to listen to us.

VELMA   You mean those other women . . . I mean, didn't those other girls ever want to listen to you, Frankie? I mean the ones who used to come here?

FRANKIE   Never! That's the trouble, Velma.

VELMA   They just wanted to talk about themselves, huh?

FRANKIE   That's it, Velma. That's exactly it.

VELMA   And that's why you're not married yet, huh? Because maybe you can't find a girl who'll listen to you?

FRANKIE   Yeah, maybe it's one of the reasons . . .

VELMA It's so hard to believe that you're not married, though. I think you'd make a nice husband and be a good father, too.

FRANKIE (*Sharply*) Why would I make a nice husband and be a good father?

VELMA (*Jittery again*) Well . . . because your kids would have so much fun with you. You'd make them laugh and everything. I never really had a father to make me laugh and have fun with because I hardly remember him.

FRANKIE You're making me feel good, Velma. In a way, you're making me feel sort of happy. You see, about a year ago around this time I almost got married. I had this girl friend, and . . .

VELMA Was she pretty?

FRANKIE It doesn't really matter now. It's not important anyway. Her name was Carrie and we went together for over a year. Then she wanted to get married. I didn't. Remember, Velma: I have a very hard time just taking care of myself. Well, anyway, that's all she talked about was getting married. In a church. The whole works. And having lots of babies afterwards. It scared me, Velma. She was ashamed now. She didn't think we should go on living together. (*He laughs bitterly*) We had to make it all legal! Carrie said some pretty stupid things to me. I was beginning to feel nervous and miserable. "Frankie Basta," she screamed at me, "you're not a man! You can't face up to responsibilities!" Over and over again she said this to me. Christ, Velma, I couldn't even take care of myself then. Almost like now: no job, no prospects, no nothing. And I didn't know whether I was a good poet or a bad one. I still don't know. And so, I asked her to try and understand. I knew I would fail her then. I said to her, "Please, Carrie-baby, just hold on and wait, and then we'll see, Carrie-honey . . . we'll see, okay?"

VELMA　But she didn't, huh?

FRANKIE　Didn't wait, you mean? No, she didn't wait and she wouldn't see. You can't do it, Velma, you can't do it! It's almost impossible to make people understand certain things, especially the people who you care so much about, the people who you love . . . or the people who you could care about and love . . .

VELMA (*Softly*)　I . . . don't know what to say to you.

FRANKIE　You don't have to say anything, Velma. Just keep me company, that's all. (*He goes to the phonograph*) What would you like to hear? Do you have any favorite songs, Velma?

VELMA　I like the one you played a little while ago.

FRANKIE　No, I mean one of your own. Don't you have one of your own favorites? That's *my* favorite song.
　　　(*There is a short pause*)

VELMA　Well . . . it's *mine*, too . . . now.
　　　(*She smiles faintly at him*)

FRANKIE (*Smiling back*)　Then I'll play it again, for the both of us.

VELMA　It would make me happy, Frankie . . .

FRANKIE　What's the matter all of a sudden? I thought you *were* happy.

VELMA　I am . . . but I'm also worried . . . and . . . I'm getting tired . . . I'm feelin' weak and everything . . . (*The music begins to play softly*) Oh, that's so nice . . . it makes me forget . . . things . . . easier . . .

FRANKIE   And you're not trembling any more, either, are you?

VELMA   Geez, you're right! I never even thought of it.
(*He has somehow managed to get her to dance with him. It is all rather awkward: his drunkenness, her fear*)

FRANKIE (*Singing, dancing*)   "Are the stars out tonight? ...I don't know if it's cloudy or bright! ...'Cause I only have eyes for . . . YOU!"

VELMA (*Pulling away, embarrassed*)   This picture of you and your family sure is nice, don't you think? Don't you think so, Frankie?

FRANKIE (*Singing*)   "Dear Velma . . . Oh, the moon may be high . . ."

VELMA   . . . and you can tell that you're different from the rest of them. I mean, you look like an artist and everything . . . all the rest of them look nice and ordinary . . .

FRANKIE (*Singing*)   "Maybe millions of people go by"

VELMA   . . . but you really stand out in the picture! You look nice and . . . *wild!* If you know what I mean? Frankie? Please, don't sing to me any more, please! I'm getting to feel scared and I can't think when you keep singing to me like that, please!

FRANKIE (*He turns off the phonograph*)   I'm sorry, Velma. Look, anything to make you cozy.

VELMA   Boy oh boy, you really are drunk, aren't you?

FRANKIE   Why do you say . . . that?

VELMA   Well, because you're acting so funny.

FRANKIE   I know, I know . . . Velma. Look, from here on in . . . well, just don't mind me too much . . . excuse me if I seem . . . in any way clumsy to you, okay?

VELMA   Frankie?

FRANKIE   Let me have your coat. I'll hang it up for you.

VELMA (*Motionless*)   Frankie, I'm getting a tiny headache . . . do you think, Frankie, that you could keep a secret? I've never been so worried . . .

FRANKIE   C'mon now: your coat?

VELMA   Yes . . .

(*She hands her coat to him.* FRANKIE *goes and puts the coat on a hanger. He notices a newspaper half-exposed in one of the pockets*)

FRANKIE (*Looking at it*)   Velma, why are you reading a newspaper like this?

VELMA   You're mad again, aren't you?

FRANKIE   How can you waste money this way?

VELMA   I buy it for my mother. She reads it.

FRANKIE   I don't want to hear another word about your MOTHER! Do you hear me?

VELMA (*Beginning to tremble again*)   Yes, yes, Frankie.

FRANKIE   Yeah, sure! You buy this rag for your old lady, but you read it too, don't you?

VELMA   It . . . has lots of gossip in it . . . about all the stars and the celebrities . . . and *everything!*

FRANKIE (*Reading*)   "Mother Uses Daughter's Head For Hammer!" (*He rips the newspaper up with great fury*)

Velma, why do you read such shit? What are you trying
to do to yourself? (*Angrily*) "Mother Uses Daughter's
Head For Hammer!" (*He moves closer to her*) God,
Velma, I mean what's happening?

(*He makes an attempt at embracing her*)

VELMA Please, please, please! Oh, nooooooo! I'M
SCARED OF YOU! I'M SCARED OF EVERYBODY,
OF EVERYTHING! (*She tries to run from him*) I never
thought of it 'til now . . . they'll do somethin' to me,
won't they? I want my coat back! I'VE NEVER BEEN
ALONE WITH A MAN BEFORE! My mother would
think . . . *my mother!*

FRANKIE (*Violently*) FUCK YOUR MOTHER! YOUR
MOTHER IS ROTTEN!

VELMA I can't stay here tonight! Maybe it jist isn't right
for me to stay here with you . . . not tonight!

FRANKIE You've got to now. You're in no shape to go anywhere. It'll be all right, Velma. You'll sleep in my bed,
and I'll sleep here on the floor. Nothing hard about that,
is there?

VELMA I can't, Frankie! *I've . . . got . . . to . . . be
. . . there!*

FRANKIE What are you talking about? (*He moves toward
her again, his arms outstretched*) Please, just let me hold
you and whisper in your ear, Velma?

VELMA NOOOOOOO! (*She pulls a small kitchen knife
out of her pocketbook. It is partly caked with dry blood*)
YOU STAY AWAY FROM ME! I DON'T WANT YOU
TO TOUCH ME! We're not even married yet . . .
(*She is trembling as she holds the knife at* FRANKIE) You
leave me alone, Frankie . . . or I'll *kill* you! (FRANKIE *is*

motionless) When . . . we got up this morning, my mother and me, we had coffeecake and caviar for breakfast. It was a big surprise. My mother said that we were havin' the treat even if payday was three days away yet. She said it was sort of a special celebration. My mother said that she was leaving for the mountains this afternoon. She was going to a resort to meet a man. Harriet, my mother's friend who lives in the next apartment, she told my mother that there were a whole lot of available men at this certain resort up in the mountains, the Catskills, I think, and my mother said she was goin' no matter what, and that I must send her money every weekend until she has some luck. She said that I couldn't go because I would scare the men away, that I would ruin her chances, and that I was really such an ugly girl, and that I looked like the mother and she looked like the daughter . . . and then she said that was why we're havin' the treat early: to celebrate! The coffeecake and caviar . . . and then she asked me to cut her a big piece of the coffeecake and to cover it with a whole lot of caviar . . . and so I started to cut the coffeecake with this here knife, but . . .

(VELMA *trembles to such a degree that the knife falls from her hand and onto the floor. She runs to the bed and throws herself upon it in a burst of hysterical sobbing*)

FRANKIE   Velma, what have you done?
(*He picks up the knife and lies it on his desk*)

VELMA   It's my mother's blood! I didn't know what to do. I don't . . . know why I did it! I don't even really remember that much, Frankie. When I got in the subway to come to work afterwards it was jist like nuthin' happened, nuthin' at all! But do you know? I thought, I thought when my mother asked me to cover her piece of coffeecake with a whole lot of caviar, I thought . . . my mother . . . she thinks that my head is a *hammer!* That's what she thinks! AND IT ISN'T! IT ISN'T! Tell me, Frankie, please tell me that my head is not a *hammer!*

FRANKIE (*After a pause*)   No, Velma, no. Your head is *not* a hammer.

VELMA (*A brief pause*)   Can I sleep here tonight?
(FRANKIE *goes to the bottle and takes the longest gulp he can manage. He falls, exhausted, down into a chair. He closes his eyes*)

FRANKIE   Sure . . . Velma.
(VELMA *continues to sob on the bed, but it is growing softer now.* FRANKIE *gets up and turns off all the lights. The moon is shining in through one of the windows*)

VELMA (*Very quietly*)   What will they do to me? I'm scared, Frankie . . .

FRANKIE   They're not going to do anything . . . to you. I'll make sure of that . . .
(FRANKIE *goes and sits down at his desk. He begins to scribble swiftly on a piece of paper*)

VELMA (*Vaguely*)   It makes me sleepy . . . alcohol . . . makes me sooooo tired . . . I've never felt soooo . . . tired . . . before in my whole life . . . (*She is no longer crying*) Help me . . . help me . . . help . . . me . . .

FRANKIE (*Still writing*)   Yes, yes . . . *I will*, Velma Sparrow . . . I promise you that *I will.*
(VELMA *is breathing heavily now.* FRANKIE *continues to write with great speed. He stops and then begins to read*)

FRANKIE (*Aloud, with a strange sobriety*)
"Dead birds still have wings
Dead birds, saddest-looking things
Because they are dead, on the ground
With their still wings, on the ground
Saddest-looking things
Dead birds with still wings,
Dead on the ground
Instead of the sky . . . "
(VELMA *is sound asleep; her breathing is peaceful.*
FRANKIE *turns and faces* VELMA's *weary and forlorn
figure. His eyes are full of tears. He stands up and
lights a cigarette*) I have a treat for you in the morn-
ing, Velma. (*He turns out the desk lamp*) I've just
written you . . . a valentine.

Curtain

Lunchtime

THE PEOPLE OF THE PLAY

AVIS, 25

REX, 27

WHERE THEY ARE

AVIS's bedroom in Greenwich Village.

When the curtain goes up the bedroom is empty. A record is dropping into place on the phonograph turntable.
It begins to play a song called "The Last Dance," sung by Frank Sinatra.

AVIS (*Entering*) Everything that needs to be done is all here, in my bedroom.

REX (*Following her in*) Yeah. Okay. (*He looks around*) But the rug . . .

AVIS You don't sound too enthused . . .

REX . . . the rug is going to give me a hard time.

AVIS Oh, dear. Well, I suppose you can be extra careful.

REX You suppose, huh?

AVIS What I meant was, I am sure you know what you're doing.

REX (*Still unfriendly*) Yeah, sure. Sure I'm sure I know what I'm doing. I also don't like what I'm doing.
     (AVIS *is getting nervous now. She goes to the phonograph*)

AVIS Is this too loud for you?

REX No. Turn it up. I like Frank.

AVIS Yes. He's marvelous, isn't he?

REX   I like the song too.

AVIS   "The Last Dance."

REX   It's too short, though. Not like a regular record. Half the length. Why do they do things like that?

AVIS   Perhaps it was deliberate.

REX   You mean on purpose.

AVIS   They don't want to spoil us.

REX   I've never been spoiled in my whole life. (*He looks around the bedroom*) You have, though, haven't you?

AVIS   I have what?

REX   You've been spoiled, right?

AVIS   (*Uneasily*)   I . . . don't really know . . .

REX   This is some place you got here.

AVIS   Thank you.

REX   What do you call places like this?

AVIS   Uh . . . apartments, I suppose.

REX   No, no, lady. I mean places that have staircases. You know, two floors.

AVIS   Oh, you mean a duplex.

REX   That's it.

AVIS   Isn't that terrible?

REX   What?

AVIS   The record's stopped already. It's really a teaser.

REX (*Looking over her body*) Uh, yeah . . . a teaser . . .
    (*She notices his attention*)

AVIS (*Nervously*) Yes . . . well . . . it's just too short.

REX We've been through that.

AVIS Anyway, I believe we had better get down to business. I realize how valuable your time must be. Now this is what I would like done. It really isn't very much. The dressing table and the chair that goes with it. And that's all.

REX Nothing else?

AVIS No. You don't mind, do you?

REX Mind what?

AVIS Well, I haven't anything else to give you.

REX You don't, huh?

AVIS I mean, there's nothing else I want you to do. I am sorry that it isn't a bigger job.

REX Is it okay if I have a cigarette?

AVIS Of course it's okay. I'll have one with you.

REX You know, I shouldn't even have asked you.
    (*He lights her cigarette, then his own*)

AVIS (*Puffing*) Thank you. Asked me what?

REX I was asking for permission.

AVIS Oh?

REX Who needs permission? I don't.
    (*He sits down*)

AVIS Yes . . .

REX You see? I didn't ask to sit down, did I?

AVIS No . . .

REX What do you think?
(*He smiles*)

AVIS Think about what?

REX Do you think maybe I should ask for permission to take my coat off?

AVIS You have a strange sense of humor.

REX Yeah, I know.

AVIS Then you're going to do the job today?

REX How come you asked that?

AVIS Well, because you've brought your equipment with you. (*She points*) That is your equipment, I take it.

REX That's right. All in this little shopping bag. Can't afford anything else to carry it in right now.

AVIS Then are you going to begin today?

REX Yes. Usually I come and give an estimate first. But I've found out that that wastes time. Now I bring my tools with me just in case the job isn't that hard.

AVIS Then this will be easy?

REX Yep.

AVIS Wonderful.

REX You haven't asked me how much it's going to cost.

AVIS Yes, please, what will it come to?

REX   You'd better go a little more into detail. Then I'll give you a price.

AVIS   Well, I want all that paint removed. On the dressing table and the chair that goes with it. I want it down to the wood itself. The natural wood . . .

REX   You want a natural finish.

AVIS   Yes, that's it.

REX   Good . . .

AVIS   I want to be able to see the wood again. It's chestnut, and . . .

REX   Chestnut. Yeah, it figures . . .

AVIS   Chestnut, and it has the most beautiful grain you've ever seen. I want to be able to look at it again.

REX   Sure . . .

AVIS   It's such a waste—covered up like that.

REX   Why did you have it painted in the first place?

AVIS   I don't really know . . .

REX   None of them know.

AVIS   Oh?

REX   Every apartment I ever go to on a job—this is the first duplex, by the way—every single one of the dames I meet in these places: they've covered up real fine good natural wood—oak, teak, walnut—with thick globs and globs of lousy paint spoiling everything. Layers and layers of it. Coat upon coat. It makes me feel *sad*, you know? Why do women always seem to want to do that? Wood from the nice-looking cherry tree, wood from the nice-looking birch tree. And then, there's the really nice-looking wood of the dying *chestnut* tree . . . you know, like the chestnut wood you got covered up underneath that dressing table of yours and the chair that goes with it. It makes me very mad: what's happened to the chestnut tree. But right now there's nothing anyone can do about it. There are hardly any left any more: the chestnut tree. Sooner or later they will all be gone. You see, they found out that the chestnut tree had this germ, and it was pretty deadly, it has some kind of poison . . . and it was spreading around underneath the ground to the roots of the other trees, the innocent ones, infecting them too. And so they're getting rid of all the nice-looking chestnut trees in order to save all of the other trees. In a couple of more years there won't be a one left nowhere in the whole wide country. And chestnut wood will be rare and expensive and . . . in a way, more nice-looking—more beautiful —than it ever was before.

AVIS   It *is* sad, isn't it?

REX   Yeah, yeah, yeah, lots of things are sad in this world going on every second of the day, and lots of people, most people, never even find out about them, and they should, you know what I mean?

AVIS   Yes . . .

REX   Well, anyway, anyway . . . where was I? I forget so easy lately.

AVIS   I think, before the dying chestnut tree, I believe you were going to talk about the various apartments you go to . . .

REX   Yeah, that's it. You're listening, aren't you?

AVIS   Yes, I am . . .

REX   Good. Well, anyway. I was going to tell you about this last place I was at a couple of weeks back. It was on the East Side, Seventy-second Street—real money too—and this lady of the house—beautiful woman, and still pretty young—she wanted me to refinish every single piece in her bedroom. The bed, the dresser, the nightstands, the dressing table and (*He smiles*) the chair that goes with it. (AVIS *smiles with him*) Everything. And they were just covered with thick coats of paint: four coats, to be exact. And each coat had been a different color. And do you know why? (*He shows her four fingers*) Because she had been through four different husbands. Four men. A coat of paint for each one. A different color for each one. "Get it down to the natural wood again," she said to me. "Get it to look the way it was originally: a natural finish is what I want." And I looked at her and then I said, "In other words, lady, what you're looking for is a *natural piece* again—am I right?" (AVIS *turns away from him.* REX *smiles*) You blush easily, don't you?

AVIS   I really believe we had better get back down to business.

REX   I've got the whole afternoon yet. What time is it now?

AVIS   It's almost noon.

REX   Yeah. I guess I'd better get started.
       (*He rises. There is a pause. He begins to take equipment out of his shopping bag*)

AVIS (*Finally*)   What were the colors?

REX (*Looking up*)   The colors?

AVIS   Yes. The four different colors. What were they?

REX   Well, I'll tell you something, you probably wouldn't
      think I'd remember, but I do. You see, while I was doing
      the job I tried to figure out what each guy was like; you
      know, each one of her husbands in relation to the color
      of paint. I force myself to do things like this, play private
      little games with myself whenever I'm in the middle of
      one of these refinishing jobs, because, like I told you be-
      fore, I don't like what I'm doing. I've got to make the
      time pass somehow, otherwise I'll blow my brains out.
      So anyway, I figured out that the first husband must have
      been the shining light of her life, her first true love, be-
      cause the color was a soft white type of thing. The second
      color was a fantastic shade of bright red. I figured that
      that husband must have been a pretty passionate guy.
      He must have worn her out because the next color was
      a dainty sort of pink, and so I figured it out that that hus-
      band must have been a faggot. And then there was color
      number four, the color I walked in on, staring me in the
      face. Jesus, you should have seen it. I had it figured out
      right away: husband number four must have been a real
      shit. Excuse my language, but that's the way I am when
      I have to make a point. (AVIS *has been laughing by now*)
      I mean, he must'uve been, because that's what the color
      was: a real raunchy shade of shit brown, and a little bit
      of shit-colored rust, too. (AVIS *is trying not to laugh now*)
      Anyway, she paid me a lot of money for that job.

AVIS Would you like anything to eat before you begin? It
      is almost lunchtime. Can I get you a sandwich and some
      coffee?

REX   I'd rather have a drink.

AVIS This time of day?

REX   Why not?

AVIS It won't affect your work?

REX   I'll do a better job, believe me.

AVIS   What would you like, then?

REX   You got Scotch?

AVIS   Yes.

REX   J and B?

AVIS   No, I'm sorry. Teacher's . . .

REX   It's good enough.

AVIS   How do you drink it?

REX   Straight.

AVIS   You're very easy to please.

REX (*Quietly*)   We'll see . . .

AVIS   What did you say?

REX   Forget it. I talk to myself a lot too.
(*AVIS exits. REX goes and puts the same record back on. He lights up a new cigarette, inspects the place very carefully, glances around and then out the windows, goes to the bed and sits on it. He bounces a few times. The bed passes his "test." He gets up and goes to where his equipment is; he spreads a lot of newspapers on the floor around the dressing table. AVIS returns with a bottle of Scotch and two glasses*)

AVIS   I've decided to join you.

REX   You mean you're going to help me?

AVIS   Oh, heavens no. I wouldn't know what to do. I'd simply be in your way. I meant that I was going to join you with a drink.

REX   That's nice. You drink Scotch too.

AVIS   Yes. George got me used to it.

REX   George your husband?

AVIS   Yes.

REX   Do you think I'm married?

AVIS   Well, I don't know. You're not wearing a ring. Of
       course, that's no way of telling, is it?
       (*She hands him a glass filled with Scotch*)

REX   You're generous.

AVIS   Oh, I'm sorry. Did I give you too much?

REX   It's perfect.

AVIS   You put Frank back on, didn't you?

REX   "The Last Dance."

AVIS   Actually, it's a rather sad song, isn't it?

REX   It can be pretty depressing.

AVIS   I suppose it all depends on one's frame of mind at the
       time.

REX   How's yours?

AVIS   What? Oh, my frame of mind? Well, now it's fine.

REX   Mine too. So the music isn't depressing.

AVIS   You're right. It isn't.

REX   So what do you think?

AVIS   About what?

REX   Am I married or not?

AVIS   I've been under the impression that you're single.

REX   (*Laughing with a tinge of bitterness*)   I've been under the impression that I'm single too.

AVIS   So you're married, then?

REX   Yep.

AVIS   (*Urgently*)   Do you have any children?

REX   Yep.

AVIS   How many?

REX   One . . . thank God . . .

AVIS   Oh? Why do you say that?

REX   Say what?

AVIS   You said "thank God" as though you were relieved at having only one child.

REX   That's right.

AVIS   (*Uneasily*)   Oh . . . I see.

REX   So what's wrong with that?

AVIS   What do you have—a boy or a girl?

REX   A boy.

AVIS   A little boy.

REX   A little boy.

AVIS   That's very nice.

REX   A little boy. And he's beautiful.

AVIS   I'm sure he is.

REX Scotch tastes good.

AVIS How old is he? Your little boy?

REX He'll be two next month.

AVIS How lovely.

REX You don't have any kids, do you?

AVIS No . . . no. I don't have any children. Not now anyway. But we're planning on it.

REX Oh, yeah . . .
      (*There is a short pause*)

AVIS How did you know?

REX Know what?

AVIS How did you know that I didn't have any children?

REX It's easy to tell.

AVIS What do you mean?

REX Look, I'm a very honest guy, see? I say what I think,
you know what I mean?

AVIS (*Tensely*) Then say it! Say what you think . . .

REX You're dyin' to have a kid.

AVIS (*Going to one of the windows and looking out*) This
little noontime meeting, this lunchtime loafing, is turning
into—into a double game, don't you think? "What's-
wrong-with-you?" and "What's-wrong-with-me?" With a
little bit of good old tingling Scotch—straight and strong
—to make things a whole lot easier.
      (*She begins to laugh*)

REX   It's not so funny. (*Then lightly*) But laugh anyway. Why the hell not?

AVIS (*Turning to face him*)   Yes, why the hell not?
(*She laughs*)

REX   You got a good laugh.

AVIS   All I did was to ask for a refinisher. Someone—a man who knows his trade, his craft well, and who would do the job right here: upstairs in the bedroom of my duplex. The people in the antique shop around the corner suggested you . . .
(*She drinks*)

REX   So?

AVIS (*Smiling*)   Well . . . look what's happened!

REX   So far, nothing's happened.
(*He drinks*)

AVIS   We've become . . . friends. That's what's happened.

REX   Anything wrong with that?

AVIS   No. No, nothing at all . . . (*She finishes her drink. They both pause without saying a word. Then* AVIS *goes to her dressing table*) Well, no matter, we'd better get down to business. (*She stops*) It's Rex, isn't it? Your first name?

REX   That's it. Rex.

AVIS   Well, anyway, this is what I would like done, Rex . . .

REX   It means "king" in Latin . . .

AVIS   Rex?

REX   That's it: Rex . . . king.

AVIS Oh? Well, I'll bet you've forgotten my first name, haven't you, Rex?

REX Nope.

AVIS What is it then?

REX Ava.

AVIS There, you see? You did forget. But you're close. Why don't you try again?

REX I don't like guessing games.

AVIS It's Avis . . .

REX Avis.

AVIS You were thinking of Ava Gardner, weren't you?

REX And what's wrong with that?

AVIS Oh, nothing. I would love to look like Ava Gardner.

REX You're putting yourself down. Listen, if Ava Gardner ever got a good look at you she'd think she was nothing.

AVIS Thank you, Rex. (*Walking impatiently*) God, would you be nice to have around the house every day at noontime. I'd never hate myself, would I?

REX I don't know.

AVIS I'm going to have one more drink with you, and then I'll leave you to yourself. Is that all right?

REX If you think so.
(AVIS *pours them both another drink*)

AVIS Here you are, Rex.

REX Thanks, Avis.

AVIS   Are you still worried about the rug?

REX   I'll need more newspapers, that's all. Do you have them?

AVIS   Oh, more than enough.
(*She heads toward the door*)

REX   Where are you going?

AVIS   To get the newspapers. They're right in the closet outside the door.
(*She stops and begins to laugh*)

REX   Now what's so funny?

AVIS   Well, you never really did get around to taking off your coat, did you? Would you like to ask for permission?

REX (*Taking it off*)   Yeah. Well, you got me thinking about all kinds of other things, Avis.

AVIS   Here. Give it to me. I'll hang it up in the closet.
(*She glances quickly down at his crotch. His fly is wide open, but he is not aware of it. She takes his coat, and then she begins to exit fast—with a slight smirk on her face.* REX *stretches widely. He walks around the room like a proud strutting peacock. He sits down at the dressing table with his drink and then looks at himself in the mirror. He pushes back his hair and then examines his teeth*)

REX (*Calling*)   So you want this dressing table and the chair that goes with it down to its natural wood again, huh?

AVIS (*Offstage*)   Yes. You see, it means a lot to me: the dressing table and the chair that goes with it. (*Returning with a bundle of newspapers*) I've had them both since the very day I was married. They were an extra-special little gift from George. I was so pleased then. George was very thoughtful, and I was so touched by it all.

REX   And so it's got sentimental value to you, right?

AVIS (*Placing the newspapers on the floor*)   Yes. I know it probably sounds rather cliché to you, but it's true.

REX   And it was chestnut wood?

AVIS   Yes, I remember it quite well.

REX   And you had it painted this color of white after what's-his-name gave it to you . . .

AVIS   George.

REX   George.

AVIS   I'm like your lady friend up on East Seventy-second Street, I suppose.

REX   You're nothing like her. She was cold.

AVIS   Oh, I see. Well, anyway, it is a soft white-type color, isn't it? And you were right, you know. It does represent —how did you put it?

REX   The shining light of her life . . . her first true love.

AVIS   Well, that's it then. With my husband George, I mean. It's exactly the same thing.
  (*There is a short pause*)

REX (*Drinking*)   But it isn't any more.

AVIS (*Turning from him*)   You can be very rude.

REX   I don't go for making believe. I don't like fooling people, and I don't like people fooling me. Do you understand what I'm trying to say? So far we've been pretty honest with each other. Why should you bother to protect your old man George? I knew what was happening to you five minutes after I walked into this place.

AVIS   That's the trouble. You know too much; you see too much.

REX   I know exactly what's going on. (*He gets up*) You've got the same thing happening up in your brain that's happening up in mine. (*He looks at his wrist watch*) This very minute: we've both got the same thing going. (*He pauses*) I like it—what I've got going. How about you, Avis? Do you like what you've got going?

AVIS   You shouldn't be doing this sort of work. You have such incredible insight. You should put it to use. You could make an awful lot of money, and you could make a tremendous amount of people happy.

REX   You're getting mad. And you're getting sarcastic. And you didn't answer my question, Avis-baby.

AVIS   I forgot it already.

REX   I can answer it for you.

AVIS   I would be disappointed if you couldn't.

REX   Do you want me to?

AVIS   Now you're asking for permission. You don't do things like that, remember?

REX   When I first entered this—duplex—your blouse (*He points*) was buttoned up to your neck . . . (AVIS *puts her hands up to her breasts*) And then you left to get the Scotch. When you came back the top button was unbuttoned. You left again to hang up my coat. When you returned with the newspapers the middle button was unbuttoned. I see where your blouse—pretty nice-looking blouse too—I see where it only has three buttons in all. (*Smiling*) Two down and one to go. (AVIS *buttons her blouse again*) And that, my beautiful and dear young lady, is the answer to the question I asked you in the beginning.

AVIS   It was warm in here. I had to cool off. And liquor certainly isn't much help, and either are you.
    (*She glances down at his fly and walks away giggling*)

REX   (*Looking down*)   Holy Christ! (*He zips it up fast*) Why didn't you tell me my fly was opened?

AVIS   (*Laughing*)   I was going to wait until it got to a crucial moment.

REX   Now I didn't do this on purpose—I mean, the way you did your blouse.

AVIS   I can't believe that you're blushing. It's lovely.

REX   These are my work pants. They're pretty old.

AVIS   (*Suggestively*)   Oh, I'm sure they're your *work* pants. And I'm sure they're *old*—they're worn-out from just too too much of *that* kind of *work* you're talking about! Oh, God, I'm really getting drunk!

REX   That's *not* work, what you have in mind. That's pleasure! (*He pours himself more to drink*) PLEASURE! Shall we drink to that? To pleasure?

AVIS   I'm getting drunk.

REX   (*Devilishly*)   Mmmmmmmm . . . I know. (*He drinks*) PLEASURE! (*Walking happily around, chuckling*) GODDAM IT! YA-HOO! GODDAM PLEASURE!

AVIS (*Laughing with him*) Rex . . . shhhh . . . the neighbors . . . shhhhhh.

REX (*Slowly beginning to undress himself*) My wife's name is Geraldine—I call her Gerry. I really should leave her. We've got to get a divorce. "But it's out of the question," she screams at me, all of the time, and then she goes running off in some corner of the apartment, crying her eyes out. And young Rex, my little boy—he knows something's wrong; he realizes things aren't right . . . kids sense those things! And before you know it, he's crying too, little Rex, Junior, along with his old lady over in the corner. And so what do you think I do? I go flying out of the house because I'm ready to cry too, and I'm sick, and I feel like my heart's disappeared. (*He grabs where his heart is*) I go flying out of our apartment before I go out of my mind, and then I head for the same ole' place: The Good Tavern. Yep. That's what it's called: The Good Tavern—my hangout, my special private little hiding-place. I used to drink there when I went to high school too. I go there now and I drink J and B straight, and I smoke one cigarillo after another, play the jukebox, dance a little, sometimes sing, feel a free pair of nice tits or two as they pass by me on their way to the phone booth, give a good long squeeze to any little young ass that happens to be wiggling by, heading toward the ladies' john . . . I do all of this in The Good Tavern, and I get away with it too, because you know why? Because they all like me there, they respect me, that's why. No matter, whenever I walk into the place, Benny the bartender, he turns off the TV set because he knows I don't want to watch it, that I want to hear music instead—Paul Anka, Bobby Darin, Connie Francis—and . . . (*He smiles at* AVIS) . . . Frank . . . Snots Himself . . . the Chairman of the Board—and they turn the volume up on the jukebox, as loud as I want it. They don't do things like that for any-

body else in The Good Tavern; only for me: Rex . . .
Rex the King. KING KONG!
   (*He laughs and beats his chest lightly*)

AVIS Rex . . . ? Maybe . . . ?

REX (*Continuing to undress*) How are you doing, Avis?
   (*He smiles warmly at her and then winks his eye*)

AVIS (*Melting*) Oh . . . fine . . . I believe . . . Rex.
   (REX *drinks, and then* AVIS *does too*)

REX Good . . . (*He pauses*) I wish Gerry drank . . .
like you, Avis. My wife Gerry doesn't drink; she won't
even touch a drop for celebrating or something like that.
That's another thing wrong with being married to Gerry
—just one of the many hundreds of goddam things. You'd
think she'd like a good stiff slug once in a while, just to
forget her troubles. But she hasn't gone near the stuff
since the night I knocked her up . . . before we were
married, of course. Yeah . . . that's it, Avis: we wouldn't
have gotten married otherwise. Christ, you know, it happened the first night we met . . . we didn't even know
each other really. It started at the Tuxedo Ballroom. I
picked her over all the other girls there because—well,
she's really a good-looking head, my Gerry is. And then
we went across the street to the Lorelei and we danced
our hearts out—every kind of dance you could think of—
and we were having one of the best times of our lives—
and we both were drinking. I got a little drunk and she
got a little drunk . . . and so off we went . . . the two
of us . . . flying through the middle of the night in my
bright red Thunderbird. (*He pauses*) I had a Thunderbird then—I was single, remember? Anyway, her ole'
man says to me after she tells him she's gonna have a kid,
her ole' man says: "I'll kill you if you don't marry my innocent little Geraldine." And all the time her ole' lady is

crying her ass off over in some corner of the apartment—just the way Geraldine does now. And then *my* ole' man and *my* ole' lady get together and they tell me it might be just the best thing that ever happened to me. "You gotta grow up some time, Rex," they're saying to me. "You can't be a kid all your life." For about two weeks I felt exactly like I was in a pressure cooker. *Their* pressure cooker! And do you know what they were cooking? They were cooking all of the youth out of me! They were killing everything that was young in me. No one has a right to do that! A man should be allowed to stay young his whole life. He's dead otherwise. I should have been an artist or a writer or something like that. Then maybe they'd understand a little bit more . . .

(*He sits down on the dressing-table chair and slowly takes his shoes and socks off. We hear a dog barking somewhere in the duplex*)

AVIS Oh, dear!

REX It's your little mutt.

AVIS He's not a mutt.

REX I think he is.

AVIS I forgot all about him: Prince. It's lunchtime. (*Calling toward the door*) Poor little Prince! I'll be right down, darling!

(*She sips some more of her drink*)

REX (*More to himself*) Your . . . Prince . . . is right here . . .

(AVIS *overhears this*)

AVIS (*Going to the door*) Oh, Prince, I know how hungry you must be. I'll be there in a second, sweetheart!

REX (*Still more to himself*)　Yeah . . . (*Smiling*) Your
Prince sure is *hungry*, too . . . (*He begins to take some
of the tools, etc., from his shopping bag.* AVIS *makes certain that she also overhears this; she stands at the door
without moving*) Avis? When I came in downstairs your
little doggie-woggie Prince wouldn't stop barking at me.
When you weren't looking I gave him a nice swift kick!

AVIS　That was horrible of you, Rex! How could you be so
unkind to such a defenseless little creature like Prince?
You're cruel . . . and I am . . . incredibly intoxicated
. . . to say the least . . . drunk out of my mind at high
noon! (*Beginning to giggle*) I would never have believed
it of me . . .

REX (*Preparing to take some of the paint off the surface of
the dressing table*)　Do you know? You're all alike . . .
I mean, in one sense you are . . . (*The dog barks again*)
You all have a little pet doggie, you dames do. Like the
babe on East Seventy-second Street. We were both in
bed and her dog, her little doggie-woggie, watched us
the whole afternoon. When I went to the bathroom he
followed me. Later on, about suppertime, I woke up in
her great big Hollywood bed, and I reached over with
my hand, not really looking, and guess who was lying
down next to me? Her ole' little doggie Bonaparte . . .
and not what I really thought it was in the first place.
>   (AVIS *decides to walk away from the door, trying to
>   stifle more giggling. She sits in the farthest corner of
>   the bedroom.* REX *gets up, wearing only his trousers
>   now*)

AVIS (*Not knowing what else to say*)　Do you think . . .
perhaps . . . we should open up a window? It certainly
is getting warm in here, don't you think, Rex? (*She
pauses*) I'm suddenly thinking a terrible thought. It
would be absolutely frightening if George, from out of

nowhere, showed up home unexpectedly, wouldn't it now?

REX   Your ole' man George *sounds* like he comes from out of nowhere. I know all about George. He's the one who doesn't want a kid, am I right? (AVIS *does not respond*) How long you been married, Avis?

AVIS   Five years.

REX   How old are you?

AVIS   Twenty-five.

REX   It's not right . . . unless, of course . . . George is an old man. What are you married to: some rich ninety-year-old guy?

AVIS (*Laughing sourly*)   George is probably younger than you . . . the healthy bastard! And in better physical shape too.

REX   I'm twenty-seven.

AVIS   You see? George is twenty-six.

REX   Well, then, if he don't want a kid, what are you hanging around for?

AVIS   I . . . don't really know. What are you hanging around Geraldine for?

     (REX *is brushing the paint remover on a part of the dressing table's surface*)

REX (*Swaying a little sometimes*)   After little Rex, Junior, was born Gerry left me twice—two different times—she ran back home to her ole' lady. I'd come home to the empty dark apartment, and it was the—well, I mean, this is going to sound pretty stupid to you, Avis, but it's the honest-to-God truth—it was the *smells* that were hanging around the apartment still: baby powder and baby oil, all mixed up with that real cozy smell of clean diapers or something like that . . . and it would make me want to go and hug and kiss and cuddle little Rex . . . who wasn't there. You know what I'm trying to say? I'm saying it's because of the kid. Both times I begged her to come back, and she did too. It's because of Rex, Junior, and nobody else, that makes me want to hang around. (*Very quietly*) Maybe it'll be different when he gets older . . . when he's grown up . . . (*He begins to scrape up the loose paint*) Hey! Hey, Avis: you've been screwed. George has screwed you and he's been a real sneak about it all. This is fake, Avis. This isn't chestnut. It's not the real stuff. It's imitation. I could tell right away. I'm an expert on this sort of thing. George gave you pieces of just plain ole' ordinary lumber that were stained by some guy in some manufacturing plant to look like *chestnut!*

> (REX *goes back and pours more Scotch into his glass; he takes a short sip.* AVIS *gets up and goes to him. She glances rather sadly, then bitterly, at the dressing table. She holds her glass out.* REX *pours more into it for her*)

AVIS (*After a pause, looking very lovingly at him*)　Thanks . . . Rex, Senior . . .
> (*She walks away with her drink*)

REX (*Doing a half-dance step*)　You're a bit of all right . . . okay . . . I like you . . . baby . . .
> (*He takes off his pants and then sits back down, wearing only his shorts*)

AVIS　When I first met George he was a prize catch: like the most perfect fish one could ever find in any ocean, all seven of them. All the girls wanted George . . . including me: Avis . . . bright-eyed and impressionable Avis.

I was so full of dreams, Rex . . . I was always dreaming . . . why, you have no idea, you simply could not imagine the dreams that I freely indulged in. (*She drinks*) Mommy and Daddy adored George. They won him over, and they, in turn, were won by George. George's parents are very much like mine. I came out at the Plaza and that's where George and I met for the first time. He was going to Harvard then, and I was ready to begin at Stevens. George's mommy and daddy pushed it and my mommy and daddy pushed it! Push, push, push! Right into it all! I didn't know what was happening. I've never really known what was happening. (*She drinks some more*) George says we're not ready yet for children. He says no matter how comfortable we are—and Christ Almighty, are we ever comfortable!—a family will only tie us down. We're still too young, he tells me. Children will make us old . . . we've got our whole lives ahead of us yet, he says. Hell! If you're not ready to have children when you've been married for over five years, when the goddam hell are you ever going to be ready to have them? Right, Rex? I mean now, really, what the hell! Why should anyone ever actually get married in the first place if they're not going to have children? Right, Rex?

REX (*Lifting his glass*)   Right, Avis!
    (*They both drink together*)

AVIS (*With light mockery*)   Oh, George . . . champion of everything he did . . . the perfect athlete—and in every field, mind you!

REX (*Whispering to the air*)   George sounds like a schmuck . . .

AVIS   Ohhhhhh . . . but George was the president of his class at prep school.

REX   . . . I was kicked out of P.S. 116 . . .

AVIS . . . and he graduated with top honors from Harvard . . .

REX . . . and so I went to Manual Training in Brooklyn . . .

AVIS . . . and very soon now, George will be the youngest president in the history of the corporation . . .

REX . . . I do refinishing myself . . .
(*They both stop now; they look at each other for a moment.* REX *moves slowly up to her; they kiss briefly and then* AVIS *moves away*)

AVIS Are you happy?

REX I'm flying, baby. How about you?

AVIS I'm flying with you, Rex.

REX (*Going toward her*) Then come back here, baby . . .

AVIS (*Running from him, laughing*) But the room is getting crowded . . .

REX (*Slowly following after her*) But you know what the radio station says . . .

AVIS (*Still moving, laughing*) No. What does the radio station say?

REX (*He stops and sings*) "You're never alone in New York . . ."

AVIS (*Out of breath*) I must make it a point—next time—to listen to your radio, Rex . . . really!

REX (*Sitting on the floor, leaning against the foot of the bed*) You do that, baby. You make it your point. (*Silence*) You nervous?

AVIS   Why do you ask that?

REX   You look nervous.

AVIS   But there's nothing to be nervous about.

REX   You sure about that?

AVIS   Positive.

REX   Good. That's the way I like to hear you talk . . .
        (*Prince is heard barking again*)

AVIS (*Rising*)   I'd better go feed him.

REX   Sit!

AVIS (*Obeying*)   Yes, sir.

REX   Good little girl.

AVIS   But it *is* lunchtime, you know . . .

REX   I know . . .

AVIS   Prince won't stop barking until I give him his lunch.

REX   How come you don't have a cat?

AVIS   Why do you ask that?

REX   A nice little kitty-kat . . . how come you don't have
        one? I mean, instead of a dog.

AVIS   I don't know why.

REX   Dogs should be pets for men, you know . . . and cats
        should be pets for women. That's the way I always think
        of it.
        (*Prince barks some more*)

AVIS   He's really an impatient little doggie, isn't he?

REX He sure *is,* baby!
     (*He imitates the dog barking*)

AVIS Are you positive you don't want me to fix you some-
      thing for lunch? I could make you nice hot vegetable
      soup . . .

REX I don't like vegetables.

AVIS Well, hot clam chowder then?

REX Too many vegetables in clam chowder too.

AVIS I could give you just a plain broth . . .

REX Don't want it . . .

AVIS . . . I have both chicken or beef. You see, you have a
      choice.

REX I don't want a choice.

AVIS Oh. Well, what about a sandwich, then?

REX You're just looking for an excuse to get out of here,
     huh?

AVIS Would you like ham? Or ham and cheese? Or a triple-
      decker with everything? On toast? Would you like a
      triple-decker with everything on toast? That sounds good
      and filling, doesn't it? And I could give you some freshly
      made potato salad with it. I'm rather ashamed to confess
      that I didn't make it myself, though. I bought it at a deli-
      catessen. Oh, and I could give you some pickles. I have
      sweet ones and sour ones. And relish! Do you like relish?
      I could give you that too. And afterwards I could give you
      a wonderful piece of freshly made apple pie. I'm rather
      ashamed to admit that I didn't bake it, though. I got it
      at the bakery this morning. Delicious apple pie, with
      vanilla ice cream, if you like. And coffee. I'll even go

down and make you a whole pot of freshly brewed hot coffee. Usually we only drink instant coffee around here. George never seems to have the time to wait for the coffee to perk. Oh, I almost forgot! Tuna fish! What about that? Would you like a tuna fish salad sandwich, maybe? A triple-decker tuna fish salad sandwich on toast with tomatoes and a little tartar sauce to go with it . . . and crispy lettuce too. Now that I could make for you myself. I'll just go downstairs and open up a can of tuna fish and I'll have the salad made in less than five minutes. Besides, I love to open up cans of tuna fish. There's something so . . . so *very real* about it . . . something so *very clean* and *natural* . . . about opening up a can of tuna fish. I suppose it's the combination of the crazy aroma that first comes from the can when you open it, and then afterward, the way in which the tuna fish looks, its color and its texture. Well, to be perfectly frank with you, it's a rather sensual experience for me . . . on the *very brink* of being sexual whenever I open up a can of tuna fish . . .
(*She is near the door now*)

REX (*Standing up*)   Yeah . . . I like tuna fish . . .

AVIS   Lovely!

REX   But forget about lunch for now, okay?

AVIS   But it will do you good. The food. The nourishment will be marvelous for you. You'll be twice as energetic for your refinishing job.
(REX *stands erect and begins to flex his muscles*)

REX (*Singing*)   "I'm Popeye the Sailor Man . . . I sleep in the garbage can." Hey, Avis, you got any spinach in the house? I'll have a great big batch of raw spinach if you got that! (*He sits on the edge of the bed*) Did you ever think of *tricking* ole' George?

AVIS (*Getting up*) But darling! (*She tiptoes by him*)
George is an *engineer!* (*Merrily*) He knows every step
of the way . . . George is methodical . . . George is
meticulous . . .

REX (*Pretending a sudden revelation*) You mean George
is careful!

AVIS Oh, God, *baby! Is he* ever *careful!* (*She points to the
bed*) I've always felt like I was on an operating table!

REX George and . . . Geraldine!

AVIS Geraldine . . . and George!

REX We should get those two together . . .

AVIS . . . arrange a meeting, I know . . .
(REX *laughs and jumps up from the bed;* AVIS *stands
over near one of the windows. They look at each
other for a moment in silence.* REX *smiles freely at
her; she is trying to relax*)

REX (*Looking around*) You know, Avis, this is a really
different world for me. Penthouses, duplexes. I like places
. . . bedrooms like this one. I feel good here . . . it's
the only time I ever actually do feel good any more, Avis
. . . when I'm in places like this one. (*He drinks*) I
dream a lot too, baby; I dream about places and people
I'd like to belong to . . . like here now . . . with you
. . . I'm a real dreamer . . . I guess that's about as far
as it goes . . . yep . . . that's about as far as it *really*
goes. (*In a much lighter mood now*) I'll tell you something, beautiful: someday . . . someday one of these
rich guys, one of these big-time husbands, is going to
murder me, I swear . . . I'll get a big barrage of blasting
bullets straight through my head. (*Beginning to laugh*)
But at least it'll be something special: I'll make medical
history. When the autopsy is finally performed . . . and

they cut open my head . . . they're going to find out that Rex the King never really had a brain at all. They're going to find a big spare *hard-on* up there instead.

(REX *then climbs into the bed: drunk and proud and still looking and behaving somewhat sober. He sits up, making himself comfortable, all the time watching* AVIS *who is now moving toward the dressing table. She sits down at it; she looks relaxed for the first time, and then she begins to dab herself with perfume. A moment passes*)

AVIS   Oh, poor George . . . so methodical, so meticulous . . . he knows every step of the way . . . five dreadful years of such dreadful caution . . . poor George and his poor plans . . . so careful . . . and so feeble . . .

REX (*After a moment*)   Avis? (AVIS *turns and faces him*) We could really fuck-up George . . . couldn't we?

(AVIS *turns back to the mirror of the dressing table. Then she gets up and disrobes down to her slip. She walks slowly toward the bed.* REX *relaxes; then he takes her down in his arms on the bed and they kiss. As the lights dim out we hear Prince barking downstairs for his lunch*)

Curtain

Halloween

HALLOWEEN *was presented by Albee-Barr-and-Wilder on October 27, 1966, at the Playwrights Unit, New York City, with the following cast:*

(*In order of appearance*)

LUKE LOVELLO   Kevin O'Connor
MARGARET MOON   Kathleen Maguire
Directed by Melvin Bernhardt

THE PEOPLE OF THE PLAY

LUKE LOVELLO,   he's going to be 30 very soon.

MARGARET MOON,   she hit 50 the other day.

WHERE THEY ARE

Manhattan: somewhere in the West Eighties off West End Avenue. An old residence-type "hotel," full of furnished rooms, trite and threadbare, with the bathrooms in the hallways; somewhat clean and tidy and quiet, but antiquated, dreary-looking, musty-smelling.

WHEN

Very late in the afternoon, a few days before Halloween; the present.

The lights slowly come up on a dismal corner of a hall-way on the third floor. LUKE *enters in the semi-light, carrying a small brown paper bag with him. He is humming quietly to himself. Then he gets louder and begins to half-sing since he is not certain of the words to the song.*

LUKE *sings something like:* "Someday she'll come along . . . The girl I love . . . And I'll be big and strong . . . For the girl I love . . . And when she comes my way . . . She'll understand . . . And everything will be okay . . . Because she's found her man . . . Her one and only man . . . The girl I love . . ."

He unlocks the door to his furnished room and then he switches on the lights. The place has been ransacked.

LUKE Hey, what the hell's going on here? (*He stands in the open doorway*) Son of a bitch! I've been robbed! (*He looks around*) Goddammitt! My clock radio is gone . . . my hi-fi is missing . . . my tape recorder's disappeared . . . my electric shoe-polisher isn't here. (*He moves in now very carefully*) My Polaroid camera! My electric razor! None of my things are here any more. (*He is suddenly tense*) Somebody's robbed me! (*He flings the brown paper bag violently up against a wall*) Someone's taken everything I own! (*He goes to the wide-opened window*) The rotten bastards! I'll kill them! (*He looks far out the window*) I'll murder them . . . I swear to shit I will! POLICE! (*He begins to search the rest of the place*) All my cuff links . . . my rings . . . my tie pins and tie clasps, my Confirmation watch and my Holy

Communion identification bracelet. If I get my hands on them I'll strangle them to death! AND I CAN DO IT TOO! (*Continuing the search*) My cigarette cases, my cigarette lighters . . . my fountain pen and pencil set! (*He runs out in the hallway*) HEY! I'VE BEEN ROBBED! CALL THE POLICE, SOMEONE, WILL YOU! (*He goes back in his room*) They came in through the window, that's it! On the fire escape! (*Out the window*) HEY, POLICE! POLICE! (*He goes and opens up the closet door and then rushes through his clothes*) My suit! My best suit! My two-hundred-dollar blue silk suit! I'll kick the bastards to death! (*He bangs the closet door shut*) Awwwwwww . . . ! For Christ's sake! For Jesus Christ's sake! (*He throws himself down on the bed*) I hope the bastards bleed to death! I hope they get hit by a car, a bus, a train. And I hope and pray to God that they suffer! (*He behaves like an impetuous child, tossing and turning and moaning and gritting his teeth on the bed, kicking and punching the pillows and the wall*) My rubber box! No, man . . . please, dear God, don't make them have taken my rubber box! (*He looks in the opened drawer of the small table beside his bed*) It's gone! They took it! My rubber box! I'LL KILL THEM! (*He runs in the hallway again*) POLICE! It was solid gold! And it had a diamond on it, and my name was engraved on the bottom of it. My . . . rubber box . . . (*He goes back into the room*) I feel just like plain goddam crying out loud, that's what I feel just like doing right now. (*He sits on the edge of the bed and puts his hands up to his eyes*) Awwwwwwwww . . . God! What did I do to deserve all of this? (*He begins to cry to himself*) Shit! That's what I say: *shit!* (*He gets up, his eyes full of tears*) Look at them! Will you just look at them all? (*He glances around at the ceiling and the walls and the floor*) Filthy cruddy cockroaches! I hate the dirty lousy crawling creepy bastards! (*He begins to attack them with his hands*) I'll fix you little shitheads now! Man, you've all had it now! (*He takes a large can from out of the brown paper bag that he threw against the wall. He begins to spray like a madman*) You don't have a chance now! None of you, you understand? (*He bangs the window shut*) Die! You miserable little pricks! Die! (*He bangs the door shut and continues to spray impulsively*) Look at them come out of their secret little nests. Hundreds of them: the mothers and the fathers and their children: their spoiled little brats. Boy, they must really fuck a lot: cockroaches! A human being doesn't have a chance. I mean, just take a good long look at them, will you? All of the expectant mothers are carrying those tiny tan-colored sacks around with them. There must be a hundred brand-new little kids inside of those tiny dragging sacks. (*He sits down on a chair in the middle of the room*) Bang, boom, CUH! Die! You lousy creepy bastards you! Die! (*He makes a long sound like a machine gun*) Drop from the ceiling, I don't care! Crawl out from the cracks up there and the light fixtures. Crawl out from the dirty woodwork and from underneath the dirty rug. I don't give a good goddam any more, do you hear me? Bang, boom, CUH! Come out for air, stupid brown shitheads, but you're still going to croak in your tracks: your fat wives are and your fat husbands are and your fat brothers are and your fat sisters are. Come out of the cruddy stove and the greasy refrigerator and the moth-infested closet and from underneath the slimy sink. I see you over there: dying on the wet water pipes, falling in that paper garbage bag full of soggy, sloshing garbage. I can just imagine them all: crawling and creeping around like crazy nuts, in and out of the pockets of my slacks and sports jackets and suits and coats in that stinking dark closet there! (*He gets up*) But not in the silk-lined pockets of my two-hundred-dollar blue silk suit, *my best suit* . . . CUSTOM MADE! . . . especially tailored for me! No, man, you sneaky guys ain't gonna die no expensive deaths in that two-hundred-dollar silk suit of mine because it ain't here any more! IT'S BEEN STOLEN! I'VE BEEN ROBBED! (*He opens the closet door and begins to shake all of his clothes wildly*) Jesus, now, will you just stand there and look at them all? Will you, now! (MARGARET *appears in the hallway. She is dressed to leave and carries a full shopping bag with her*) Before I go to sleep here tonight in this frigging rathole, I'm going to make sure that each one of you is stone dead! DO YOU HEAR ME, YOU SHITHEADS? (MARGARET *stops and turns to* LUKE's *door.* LUKE *drops back down in the chair*) I wish I had a penny, that's all, just one single penny, for every single cockroach dying here right now. I'd be rich enough to buy everything back that was stolen from me this afternoon. (MARGARET *is now listening at the door.* LUKE *gets up from the chair and lies down on his bed. He is exhausted*) They really do fuck a lot: cockroaches! They must love to do it. I love to do it . . . too! I really do! I'M TELLING YOU: I REALLY DO LOVE TO DO IT! (*He begins to sob again*) I want to . . . so much sometimes . . . I really want to! It's not fair, God, it's really and truly not fair. You know, you actually piss me off sometimes, God, you really do! (*He quiets down for a moment*) I'VE BEEN ROBBED! (MARGARET *knocks lightly on his door.* LUKE *sits up on the bed*) Who is it? Who's there?

MARGARET It's Margaret . . .

LUKE (*Getting off the bed*) Who's Margaret? I don't know anyone named Margaret.

MARGARET I'm Margaret Moon. I . . .

LUKE What do you want?

MARGARET I heard you yell for help.

LUKE   I didn't yell for help.

MARGARET   I heard you say that you were robbed.

LUKE   What do you do: listen at keyholes all of the time?
This place is giving me the creeps. I'm moving out of
here as fast as I can.
    (LUKE *goes to the door very cautiously and with
    much suspicion in his manner*)

MARGARET   Oh? I'll go . . . then.
    (*She begins to move slowly away.* LUKE *then opens
    the door; he is slow and sure and careful as he
    does it*)

LUKE   (*Peeking out*)   Who are you? What are you doing
here?

MARGARET   I'm Margaret Moon.

LUKE   You told me before.

MARGARET   Well, you asked me twice already.

LUKE   You got a phone in your room? I gotta call the
police.

MARGARET   I don't live here.

LUKE   Then what are you doing, sneaking around hallways
like this?

MARGARET   You just moved in yesterday.

LUKE   How come you know so much?

MARGARET   I work here.

LUKE   Then maybe you know something about me being
robbed.

MARGARET   I'm one of the maids here.

LUKE   The cleaning lady . . .

MARGARET   I'm a maid. I clean up the rooms in this building. I do the third floor and the fourth floor all by myself, Monday through Saturday, six days a week, from eight 'til three o'clock every afternoon, except Saturdays when I go home at noon. You won't be seeing me for the next two weeks. Dolores will be cleaning your room while I'm away on my vacation enjoying myself.

LUKE   (*His patience gone*)   I was just robbed, miss! They cleaned me out! Swiped all of the things that meant so much to me, all of the things that were worth the most money.

MARGARET   I'm sorry . . .

LUKE   And my place is full of dying cockroaches!

MARGARET   Yes, I know . . .

LUKE   I'm moving out of here tomorrow!

MARGARET   Why don't you give it all another chance? I'll be coming back in two weeks.

LUKE   They got in through the window. The window was locked when I left today. Did you open the window?

MARGARET   I . . . no . . .

LUKE   Yes, you did! I can tell!

MARGARET   Don't raise your voice to me like that.

LUKE   You're lying to me!

MARGARET   You stop that!

LUKE   You did open the window, didn't you?

MARGARET   What are you implying: that I'm a liar?

LUKE   Yes, you're a liar! I can tell!

MARGARET   Don't call me a liar, young man! And you stop that screaming at me, do you hear? If I get my Irish temper up you'll be sorry!

LUKE   Yeah? Well, I already got mine up!

MARGARET   You're not Irish. I saw your name. It's Italian.

LUKE   You know too much.

MARGARET   I happened to see it on one of your suitcases in the closet.

LUKE   Like I just said before, miss—you know too much!

MARGARET   You have no respect for other people, do you?

LUKE   I'm both, miss.

MARGARET   You're both what?

LUKE   My mother's name was O'Leary. My father's the Italian. I'm Luke O'Leary Lovello.

MARGARET   I see.

LUKE   So that's really something, don't you think? An Irish temper is bad enough. But combined with the temper of an Italian? Well, it will knock you right on your ass!

MARGARET   Watch your language with me, young man! You're not talking to just plain trash! Do you hear me?

LUKE   All right, I'm sorry . . . (*He goes down the hall-way*) POLICE!
        (*There is a short pause*)

MARGARET   I feel bad about the robbery.

LUKE   Thanks. But it doesn't do me any good.

MARGARET I did do it . . .

LUKE Do what?

MARGARET I *did open* the window.

LUKE I knew it! Now wasn't that a stupid thing to do?

MARGARET I told you not to raise your voice to me. Have some respect for your elders.

LUKE Do you want to come in? Do you want to come in and see what they took? (*He opens the door wide for her*) It will make you sick. All the things that meant so much to me: GONE! (MARGARET *enters the room with him*) The smell is going to make you sick too: cockroach poison everywhere in the air.
(*He slams the door behind them*)

MARGARET You're much too excited, young man.

LUKE Why not?

MARGARET Why don't you make a try of being calm?

LUKE Of course I'm excited and of course I'm not calm. Wouldn't you be?

MARGARET It could'uve been a lot worse, you know?

LUKE Lady, it has been a lot worse, let me tell you!

MARGARET Then why be so upset?

LUKE Do you smoke?

MARGARET No.

LUKE I don't very much either. But I need a cigarette right now.

MARGARET   Try some hot tea. It will make you feel better. It will give you a lift. It's good weather for hot tea. It's getting awfully cold out there. It's supposed to go down to thirty degrees tonight. That's very unusual for the end of October.

LUKE   I'm mad, lady, really mad! Why didn't you leave the window closed and locked the way I left it? I was warned about the daily robberies in this neighborhood. Lots of Puerto Ricans around.

MARGARET   Lots of them on the next street over.

LUKE   This is all a new experience for me. I've never been on my own before.

MARGARET   How old are you?

LUKE   I'm going to be thirty very soon.

MARGARET   Then it's about time, don't you think?

LUKE   About time for what?

MARGARET   About time that you were on your own.

LUKE   Actually, lady, it's none of your business. Did you ever think of that?

MARGARET   You're very fresh. Did you ever think of that?

LUKE   Then get out! (*He opens the door*) G'wan! Leave, lady. I don't need you around to make things worse! You're the one to blame for my being robbed. You're the responsible one, lady! C'mon now: did you ever think of that?

MARGARET   Please, please, please: don't say that. It's true. It was an accident, though. I thought I was doing what only seemed right. I opened the window to let some air in while I was cleaning up, that's all.

LUKE   All you do is make the bed and then you dust a little . . .

MARGARET   And I run the sweeper on the rug!

LUKE   Well, what good is it? You didn't get rid of the cockroaches.

MARGARET   That's not part of my job.

LUKE   Well, why not? You afraid of a few . . . a few thousand cockroaches?

MARGARET   The exterminator is coming here on Monday. He knows about your room. I put it down as first on his list. The cockroaches aren't my fault. It was the man who lived in here before you. Mr. Potter. And he would never let me in here, for a whole year he kept me from ever coming in here. He paid his rent on time, exactly, every day at nine in the morning instead of by the week. He lived like a pig. The cockroaches are his fault, not mine. And not the landlady's either.

LUKE   Yeah? Well, what the hell did he do then? Keep them as pets? It looks to me as though he fed them every day, too, on schedule, like he paid his rent so regularly. Listen, lady, I've been with the Sanitation Department of the City of New York for over ten years now, ever since I got bounced out of high school, and I ain't never seen cockroaches this big before in my whole life.

MARGARET   Are you kidding?

LUKE   Kidding about what?

MARGARET   About being a garbage collector . . .

LUKE   What's wrong with that?

MARGARET   I mean working for the Sanitation Department . . .

LUKE   I said, what's wrong with that?

MARGARET   I didn't say anything was wrong with it.

LUKE   You say it like it's an insult or something.

MARGARET   You just don't look the type, that's all.

LUKE   Well, it's all over now. I quit two days ago. I got up early in the morning and I left. I came here. And now I'm ready to get up early tomorrow morning and leave again after all of this bullshit.

MARGARET   I told you to watch your language in front of me.

LUKE   (*After a pause*)   Are you staying?

MARGARET   What do you mean?

LUKE   I'm going to close the door if you're staying. Keep the air full of poison for the cockroaches.
   (*He closes the door*)

MARGARET   I don't mind it . . .

LUKE   Sit down, if you want to . . . goddammitt!

MARGARET   What's the matter?

LUKE   I'm sorry. Sorry about the swearing again. But I'm mad. I'm really sore about my being robbed. Every time I think about it I feel I could kill someone . . .

MARGARET   I don't blame you. (*She goes to the window*) I'll open up the window just a bit . . .

LUKE   No! Don't! I don't want any of them escaping!

MARGARET (*Sitting down*) Do you know what I think? I think you should forget about the cockroaches.

LUKE Are you kidding?

MARGARET No, I'm not. And I also think you should forget your being robbed.

LUKE You *must* be kidding, lady!

MARGARET I'm not, Luke.

LUKE Forget about it! All those things—they were all I ever had. (*He begins to spray some more*) Look at them! Still coming out from everywhere. What did you say his name was?

MARGARET Whose name?

LUKE The guy who lived here before me.

MARGARET Mr. Potter.

LUKE Why did Mr. Potter move away?

MARGARET Well, it's sort of complicated.

LUKE Yeah? Well, I'll bet it was because of the cockroaches. They finally got the best of him and so he had to move out.

MARGARET Don't be smart, young man. It was because his wife died. Mr. Potter talked to me once, only once. He told me he was married for forty-five years. To the same woman. From the very day they were married to each other he said that he never had anything to do with another woman in the way of love and romance or what have you. I'm sure that he was telling the absolute truth. The day after his wife's funeral he moved out of his house without ever telling anybody. There was no warning, no indication whatsoever. He had four sons and two daughters and lots of grandchildren. He didn't tell any of them. Somehow, none of them mattered any more because his wife was dead and gone. He said that it was perfect while she was alive and she was his wife and he was her husband, but now it was all over, and she was dead and buried and in God's hands, and so nothing else mattered any more. It was over a whole year before they finally tracked him down: living here, in your room now, all by himself, like you, and always keeping to himself. That was the day he talked to me. When his youngest son, the baby of the family, had found out where he was staying. It was also the same day that he moved. Real fast. (*She gets up*) I know exactly how he felt . . .

LUKE Don't leave, please . . .

MARGARET I'm not going anywhere. I thought I would give you a hand. I'll straighten up your place for you.
(*She takes off her coat*)

LUKE There's nothing to straighten up. I don't care, you see? I'm leaving here tomorrow, just as fast as Mr. Potter did. I'm going to find another place to stay.
(*There is a pause: he looks carefully at her figure*)

MARGARET What's the matter?

LUKE Nothing's the matter. Look, what should I do? Should I try calling the police?

MARGARET It wouldn't do much good.

LUKE Yeah, I guess you're right. (*He sits down on the bed*) You know what I think, lady?

MARGARET I told you my name is Margaret Moon. I want you to call me Margaret, and I'll call you Luke.

LUKE Okay, Margaret: you know what I think?

MARGARET   What do you think, Luke?

LUKE   I think you're a good-looking head. I think you got a nice body.

MARGARET   Well, now, that's good to hear. Thank you, Luke. But you wouldn't believe it, would you? Well . . . maybe I shouldn't tell you, after all . . . it might just spoil things a little, and who wants to do that?

LUKE   C'mon, what? Tell me.

MARGARET   (*After a pause*)   I just hit fifty the other day.

LUKE   Aw, c'mon! I don't believe it! You look about thirty-five!

MARGARET   I'm fifty years, exactly three days ago. I got a boy and two girls and they're all married and they've given me six grandchildren so far . . . and I got a husband, James: James Moon.

LUKE   The world is all screwed-up, isn't it, Margaret? I mean it's full of surprises.

MARGARET   Lots and lots of surprises.

LUKE   I can't take it any more: all these surprises. All my life it's been surprise after surprise. And do you know, surprises are supposed to be good, aren't they? Surprise parties. Surprise birthday presents, Christmas presents, wedding presents, graduation presents: all surprises. (*Quickly*) Do you have a transistor radio on you?

MARGARET   What would I be doing with a transistor radio on me?

LUKE   You see, that's a surprise: everyone has a transistor radio on them nowadays. They robbed that, too—my transistor radio! It was a surprise birthday present from my favorite aunt. It cost fifty-five dollars; real leather case to it and everything. I gotta have some kind of music. I can't live without music. Look, they swiped my hi-fi, but they didn't swipe any of my records, stupid creeps.

MARGARET (*Examining the inside of the closet*)   I think I've just now figured it all out for you, Luke.

LUKE   What?

MARGARET   They dumped everything in your two laundry bags. You see what they did: they dumped all of your dirty clothes out of the laundry bags and then they left. There had to be at least two of them. It would have been too heavy for one person to be able to carry both laundry bags when you think of some of the heavy things they took. You know, Luke, I'll bet you they didn't even leave by the fire escape the way they came in. I'll bet you they left by the door right here and then walked down the stairs and out onto the streets with the laundry bags slung over their shoulders. No one even noticed them. They could'uve been just two nice laundry men doing their job. It's a shame.

LUKE   You know, Margaret, you know too much. You know just too damn much and I don't like it!

MARGARET   It's not that I know too much. It's just that I'm not stupid, that's all. It doesn't take too much brains to figure that one out anyway. I'm a wise ole' dame, let me tell you.

LUKE   You don't look as old as you say you are.

MARGARET   I told you before how old I was. I've got twenty years on you. It's been a full-time job just trying to keep myself looking young. So take it or leave it!

LUKE   You gettin' sore at me?

MARGARET   Well, you're gettin' sore at me, ain't you? Besides, I really gotta be goin'.

LUKE   Aw, c'mon.

MARGARET   Well, I don't know. I'm worried.

LUKE   What are you worried about?

MARGARET   I'm worried about you.

LUKE   Me? But what for?

MARGARET   I'm worried about your temper. It sorta scares me. Maybe it's because we don't know each other. Maybe that's why I feel this way. After all, we are strangers, really . . .

LUKE (*Looking in the closet*)   My umbrella!

MARGARET   What?

LUKE   My umbrella! They robbed that too!

MARGARET   You weren't even listening to me before . . .

LUKE   It was a damn good umbrella. It came all the way from Italy with a beautiful hand-carved handle on the top made of dark brown expensive wood. They knew what they were doing. That good black umbrella cost my old man twenty bucks the day he bought it for me. It was a surprise present from the ole' guy. He thinks it gives you a respectable appearance. He's a real old-fashioned guy, my old man. He said to me: "Luke, here's an umbrella for you. It'll make a good impression on the girls when you need to use it, in case they got a gown on and you got a tuxedo on for a formal dance, a prom or something like that." But I never really got to use the umbrella.

MARGARET (*Quietly*)   I really think I should be goin'.

LUKE   Don't.

MARGARET   It's gettin' late, Luke.

LUKE   I wish I had a smoke. I wish I had something to drink. A good stiff one would help me a little right now. I would like to be able to offer you a drink. I don't have anything here because I don't like to drink alone. I like to talk to people whenever I'm drinking. I usually drink in bars every night. I used to drink at the K. of C., you know: the Knights of Columbus. I belong to them. (*He takes the spray can in his hand*) Look at them: still coming out in droves, like dying flies.

MARGARET   No more. Please, no more.

LUKE   No more what?

MARGARET   No more spraying, Luke. Let them be. They'll die now anyway. We'll die too if we don't get some air in here.

LUKE   You dye your hair, don't you? I mean if you just hit fifty the other day then you must dye your hair.

MARGARET   Of course I do.

LUKE   Did you have much gray hair before?

MARGARET   Lots of it.

LUKE   How old were you when you started getting it?

MARGARET   It started when I was your age.

LUKE   Oh, Christ! That worries me.

MARGARET   Don't let it worry you. It comes with worry.

LUKE   It's really a surprise, the way you look for your age. It's a good surprise, though. But don't get me wrong, Margaret: there are an awful lot of bad surprises too.

MARGARET   I know, Luke.

LUKE   Like this robbery, for instance.

MARGARET   I sorta got a surprise for you.

LUKE   No kiddin'?

MARGARET   I don't know whether it's good or bad, though.

LUKE   C'mon. I'm ready for anything now.

MARGARET   (*Sitting down in the chair*)   I was lying to you before.

LUKE   You mean about the window? You already admitted that to me.

MARGARET   No, I mean about the cigarettes. Look here. (*She takes a carton of cigarettes from her shopping bag*) A whole brand-new carton of cigarettes . . . for you, Luke. It's a surprise.

LUKE   But it's a good surprise. What did you mean when you said you didn't know whether it was good or bad?

MARGARET   Well, it's not good that I lied to you the first time you asked about smoking. Like it's not good that I lied to you the first time you asked me about who opened the window. I don't like lying at all. And I hate it when other people lie, don't you?

LUKE   I usually can't sleep because of it.

MARGARET   So here are your cigarettes. You can keep the whole carton.

LUKE   Not my brand. But I still appreciate it.
(*He begins to open the carton*)

MARGARET   I bought them for James, my husband. It was
a little surprise for him. But I've changed my mind now.
It's all right, so don't worry about it, Luke.

LUKE   Would you like one?
(*He offers her a cigarette*)

MARGARET (*Taking a cigarette*)   Are you hungry, Luke?

LUKE   I don't have anything to eat here. I'm sorry there's
nothing I can give you, Margaret.

MARGARET   Not for me. I mean are *you* hungry, Luke? I've
got some roast beef with me.

LUKE (*Lighting her cigarette*)   You seem to have everything with you . . . (*He laughs softly*) In more ways
than one, Margaret. (*He lights his own cigarette*) If you
know what I mean?

MARGARET   I know what you mean. You're a flirt, that's
what you are, Luke.

LUKE (*Puffing away nervously*)   Yeah, yeah, yeah!

MARGARET   You're a hard one to figure out, you are.

LUKE (*Suddenly laughing*)   We're going to die in here together! All this deadly cigarette smoke, all the fumes of
the poisonous cockroach spray, the window shut tight,
the door closed solid, the sad smell of ole' Mr. Potter still
here in the air, my dirty sweaty clothes over there, the
stinking smell of the filthy low-down rats who robbed
my place: that's still here, too . . .

MARGARET   The radiator. You forgot about the steam and
the heat and the smell from the radiator.

LUKE   And the radiator. No air at all, Margaret Moon. Do you think you can stand it?

MARGARET   I can stand almost anything.

LUKE   I can too.

MARGARET   Here's the roast beef in case you get hungry. (*She takes it out of her shopping bag*) I made it myself. All fixed up in this big empty pickle jar with my own special thick brown gravy to go with it.

LUKE   What color was your hair before it got gray?

MARGARET   It was the same color it is now. (*Instantly*) I brought this roast beef for my lunch today. We got a little stove down in the basement here where we can fix up things to eat. I just didn't feel like eating my lunch today even though I knew how delicious it would be. Dolores kept talking on and on about how she cheats on her husband and how she loves getting away with it. Well, I'll tell you, it made me sick to my stomach. I've been married since I was nineteen years old and I never even once thought of doing anything like that, Luke.

LUKE   What's Dolores look like?

MARGARET   And I suppose this being the last day before my two-week vacation begins tomorrow also made me kinda nervous. I get two weeks off in the summer, but I never take my time off then—in the summer, I mean. I wait until the fall comes, because it's my favorite season —the autumn. (*A pause*) Don't get too acquainted with Dolores. This is a warning. She's a terror, a holy terror. She'll go for you. So be careful. I think it would be good for your own sake if you were cold to her. Just let her do her job, that's all.

LUKE (*Sitting down on the bed*) You know why you look so young? Because of the way you wear your hair. It's feminine, the way a woman's hair should be, not like the girls you see nowadays. And there are so many other things about you, too, Margaret.

MARGARET I don't wanna hear any more.
(*She gets up*)

LUKE Where are you going?
(*He gets up and touches her arm gently as if to hold her back*)

MARGARET I . . . I'm really not going anywhere . . .

LUKE Notice something?

MARGARET What?

LUKE This is the first time we've touched.

MARGARET Oh?
(*She moves away from him*)

LUKE Listen, Margaret, I didn't mean to get too personal with you or anything like that. I was just complimenting you, that's all. Look, I'm sorry, I really am, if you're insulted in any way.

MARGARET I'm not insulted at all, young man, really I'm not.

LUKE Aw, c'mon, Margaret, cut out the "young man" baloney, okay? I keep thinking we're both the same age.

MARGARET Well, I'm sure there have been lots of young girls in your life. (*She forces a laugh*) What do you want with an old bag like me?

LUKE Aw, c'mon, Margaret. Why do you have to say things like that for?

MARGARET   I'm sure you can get all kinds of young girls
. . . and I suppose that's the way it should be, Luke.

LUKE   Oh, sure, sure, it's okay, I guess. Yeah, I have been
pretty lucky. I've had the cream of the crop. I've had
more girl friends in my life already than there are cockroaches dying in this very room right now. You know, I
never went steady with any one girl, though. I liked
having a different one whenever I felt like it. Any time
I wanted to make a phone call . . . to a new one or an
old one or one I hadn't seen in a long time . . . well, I
would go ahead and do it. I've always enjoyed that sort
of life. I like being a man and proud of the way I've been
able to keep so many women on a string . . . without
the string ever breaking, too. Yeah, Margaret, I've really
been awfully lucky, let me tell you. I've never gotten
myself into any trouble either with any of these girls, if
you know what I mean. It's almost a miracle, in a way,
because I got an awful appetite when it comes to you
know what, and well, guys like me, well, we also lose
control a lot, you know, like get too passionate and wild
sometimes and not thinking beforehand. I guess I never
really got myself into trouble or any of these girls into
trouble, either, because deep down inside I'm a pretty
religious guy, and so I pray a lot too, if you know what I
mean?

MARGARET   (*After a long pause*)   I suppose I really better
be goin'.

LUKE   Don't go! Hey, what's the matter? Did I say anything wrong? I didn't upset you, did I?

MARGARET   No . . .

LUKE   Then what's wrong?

MARGARET   (*After a moment*)   It's all a *lie*, Luke.

LUKE   What?
(*He is suddenly very nervous*)

MARGARET   *All a lie.*

LUKE   What do you mean?

MARGARET   You know what I mean.

LUKE   I . . . I don't know what you're talking about, Margaret.

MARGARET   Because you don't want to know what I'm talking about, young man, that's why.

LUKE   What I just told you about all my girls, my women. You think it's all a . . . lie?

MARGARET   Yes, I do. I think it's all one big fat lie.

LUKE   Well . . . I . . . really don't care what you think!

MARGARET   I'm sorry . . .

LUKE   Besides, what you think doesn't mean a goddam thing to me, do you understand?

MARGARET   Watch your language around me.

LUKE   The hell I will now! You calling me a liar!

MARGARET   You called me one before.

LUKE   That's right, I did. And then you even admitted it.

MARGARET   Then why don't you admit it now, about yourself? Oh, sonny boy, who are you ever trying to impress? You don't have to impress me, not with lousy lies, you don't. I'm impressed with you already, just the way you are. Luke, I could see right through you. I know all about people who lie. I've been in love with a man for the last thirty years and he's spent a good deal of the last twenty of those years lying to me. I'm an expert at it, dear boy. My husband James has slept with more women than you'll ever be able to sleep with in your whole lifetime.

LUKE   While he was married to you?

MARGARET   While we were bringing up our children.

LUKE   Your husband?

MARGARET   My husband: James Moon. Ever since the day I met him, I would say to him, at least once a day: "James Moon, you make Margaret swoon." It was silly, but it was a nice way, I thought, and he did too for a long time, of saying to him: "I love you." Then, just these past few months, mind you, I found myself saying something else instead. Never out loud, though; never to him any more, but to myself. (*She smiles wryly*) "James Moon, you're such a goon." (*She pauses*) My husband, James Moon, is a no-good rotten son of a bitch!

LUKE   But you still love him?

MARGARET   I don't know . . .

LUKE   I don't think you do . . .

MARGARET   Come to think of it, maybe I don't any more! You know, in the beginning it was perfect for me, Luke, the way it was perfect for Mr. Potter. It's not so perfect any more, though. I've never done anything like this before in my whole life. I've been hanging around all afternoon since three o'clock. I don't want to go home tonight. What do you think? Do you think that maybe it has to do with hitting fifty the other day? Maybe I just have finally given up. Now that's a miracle if it's true. I'm even tired of crying about it, and God only knows how much I've cried about it all. I've always prayed too, Luke. I used to pray to Saint Jude a lot . . .

LUKE Yeah, me too . . . whenever I was desperate, Margaret.

MARGARET He's for truly desperate cases, Saint Jude, and so I really took advantage of that. And I lit so many candles, Luke. And then for a very long time it was Saint Rita because I started not to feel too well . . .

LUKE I used to pray a lot to her too. I know what you mean by not feeling too well. It has to do with the heart. Your heart, my heart. It gets sick. You know, I really do believe in that expression: a broken heart. You *can* have a broken heart. I believe that people really do die from their broken hearts. Remember when Mario Lanza died? He was so young, and what a great voice. Well, remember not too long afterward? His wife died. Just like that! And she was even younger. They just found her dead in bed one day out in Hollywood. Her name was Betty, I always remember it, and she was Irish the way my mother is, and Mario was Italian the way my father is, and good Catholics too. And the doctors really didn't know how she died . . . but I think she probably died of a broken heart. She couldn't go on living without the man she loved. Just like Mr. Potter, in a way.

MARGARET Yes . . .

LUKE Margaret, are you okay?

MARGARET Oh, I don't know . . .

LUKE I'll tell you something: I feel a little better than I did before. I guess it's our talking to each other.

MARGARET (*Quietly*) I can't go home tonight. It's the beginning of my vacation tomorrow and James will spend the whole two weeks with me like he's always done: lying, making believe. I can't take that sort of thing any more, you know what I mean, Luke? Sure,

sure, I look good . . . real damn good, even if I have
to admit it myself . . . but it was because I wanted him
to love me again, like in the beginning. I've wasted myself for the last twenty years. Maybe that's why I look
so good, huh? (*She laughs half-bitterly*) Because I've
been preserved for the last twenty years of my life, that's
why.

(*She takes a paper bag from out of her shopping bag
and then she pulls out a bunch of Halloween masks*)

LUKE What are you doing?
(*She puts one of the masks on her face*)

MARGARET Happy Halloween! I don't want you to see me
cry, that's all. I'm sparing you that because I'm impressed
with you, no matter what. Take one if you like, and put
it on too. I bought them for my grandchildren. Tomorrow night's Halloween, isn't it?

LUKE I don't know. Is it?

MARGARET (*After a pause*) Don't lie to me any more,
Luke.

LUKE (*Putting one of the masks on too*) It . . . wasn't
. . . well, they weren't lies that meant to hurt you. If
you really want to know something, they hurt me, right?
I'm hurting myself because I almost believe that I had
all those women in my life.

MARGARET I think you're a good man, Luke Lovello, I
really do.

LUKE Thanks . . .

MARGARET I never slept with another man in my whole
life. Only James Moon. He was the first . . . and there's
been no one since.

LUKE   I like your legs, Margaret.

MARGARET   What's that, Luke?

LUKE   I said I like your legs. I didn't notice them before.
You weren't wearing a mask. I go for them a lot, Margaret. (MARGARET *sits back down in the chair still wearing the Halloween mask. She lifts her skirt above her
knees and then she crosses her legs*) I got a candle here
in a wine bottle. Shall I light it? It would be sorta fun,
don't you think? Because of the Halloween masks and
everything, don't you think?

MARGARET   Go ahead and light it then, Luke.
    (LUKE *lights the candle, then turns out the ceiling
    lights. He sits on the edge of the bed facing* MAR-
    GARET *across the room. He is still wearing his mask
    too*)

LUKE   It's kinda way-out, don't you think?

MARGARET   Yes, it is, Luke.

LUKE   (*After a long pause*)   You're really . . . well, I
mean that . .

MARGARET   Go ahead, Luke, say it.

LUKE   I mean, you're really built okay, Margaret . . . (*A
short pause*) Geez, I wish we had some music . . .
    (*He gets up and begins to walk about slowly but
    nervously*)

MARGARET   You don't want me to go, do you?

LUKE   No! No, I want you to stay here with me. Margaret,
I want you to listen to me. I'm sorry that I lied to you. I'm
sorry that I thought I should give you that impression
about myself. I'm not that at all. Pardon the language,

Margaret, but I'm not that ass-man I was telling you all
about before.
> (*The light of the candle flickers as he walks about
> the room. It throws off weird and crazy shadows,
> especially over the masks they wear on their faces*)

MARGARET   Maybe you'd better forget about it.

LUKE   No, I want to tell you. I want you to listen to me.
> (*He goes to the bed again and sits back down. There
> is dead silence*)

MARGARET   I like the quiet . . .

LUKE   Yeah . . .

MARGARET   It's good for us to think a minute or two . . .

LUKE   I know . . .
> (*Another dead silence*)

MARGARET (*Finally*)   What was that?

LUKE   What was what?
> (*He gets up*)

MARGARET   Please sit back down again. Be calm.

LUKE   Okay . . .
> (*He sits back down on the edge of the bed*)

MARGARET   There . . . now be calm.
> (*Another silence*)

LUKE (*Finally*)   Are you okay, Margaret?

MARGARET   I'll be all right.

LUKE   I think the noise you heard must have been the candle: the wax melting from it and then falling down the
wine bottle.

MARGARET Yes, that's probably it.

LUKE I wish we had something to drink together, I really do.

MARGARET The smoking is good enough.

LUKE I was just thinking . . .

MARGARET Think to yourself for a few minutes more. Think about what you plan to do with yourself, with your future. Now . . . tonight . . .

LUKE I have some things to tell you first, Margaret.

MARGARET There it is again . . . that noise I heard before. Are you sure it's the wax on the candle?

LUKE (*Getting up again*) Now wait a minute . . .
       (*He begins to chuckle*)

MARGARET What are you laughing at?

LUKE (*Laughing*) Do you know what it is? It's the dying cockroaches. The little falling bastards . . . they're still dropping like flies from the ceiling. (*He begins to swat a couple of them with his bare hands*) Do you think I should spray some more, or do you think they've really had it by now?

MARGARET Oh, they've really had it by now, I'm sure of that.

LUKE What do you think about the guys who robbed me? Do you think the bastards will ever get caught?
       (*He removes the mask*)

MARGARET They deserve to be, and that means that they will be, and so don't worry about it any more.

LUKE (*Picking up another mask*)   How do I look in this one?
  (*He puts it on*)

MARGARET (*After a moment*)   It's funny. It's not a scary mask like the rest of them. It's more human, the more I look at you in it. And you look familiar now. (*Laughing quietly*) You look like someone I think I know.

LUKE   No kidding?

MARGARET   Someone famous, maybe . . .

LUKE   Yeah? Who?
MARGARET   Someone in the movies.

LUKE   Can't you think?

MARGARET   Well, in a very funny way, you look like Gene Kelly with that mask on your face.

LUKE   Honest to God?

MARGARET   You sound very happy about that.
  (*She removes her mask*)

LUKE   I suppose I am. You see, I used to be a big fan of Gene Kelly's. He was my favorite movie actor. (*He removes the mask*) I never missed one of his movies and I saw them over and over again. Hell, I always went to the movies, anyway. I loved the movies. Especially the musicals, the M-G-M musicals. I always had the money to go. My mother and father never stopped giving me money for the movies. I loved them all: Gene Kelly, Judy Garland, Esther Williams, Ricardo Montalban, June Allyson, Gloria DeHaven, Van Johnson, Jane Powell. They were the M-G-M ones. Always in beautiful Technicolor. And there was Betty Grable and June Haver. They were the Twentieth-Century Fox ones. Always in beautiful Technicolor. And then there was Rita Hayworth. She was always in the ones from Columbia. Always in beautiful Technicolor. But it was Gene, Gene Kelly, and Esther, Esther Williams: they were really my favorites. I loved them both so much. I used to dream, think a lot about being like Gene. I always imagined myself dancing in the movies. Dancing and singing the way he did. And I used to always think that M-G-M should have a male-type actor, a great swimmer, like Esther Williams, and he would be a star too, and they would play opposite each other. I used to always think that maybe I could become a star like that: a combination of Gene Kelly dancing and singing and a male-type version of Esther Williams swimming. I really loved those days when I used to go and see those pictures. You know?

MARGARET   I never went to the movies very much. I raised a big family, remember? And James was never home. I read a lot. I read all the great books. I read *Gone with the Wind, The Good Earth, King's Row, A Tree Grows in Brooklyn,* all of them.

LUKE   I never read a book in my whole life. I didn't have the patience.

MARGARET   It's too bad. It would have helped you a lot. It helped me a lot. I read all of the great authors. Mostly the women: like Faith Baldwin, for instance. And Taylor Caldwell, and Kathleen Norris. It would really help me get through the day and the night sometimes, reading their books; learning about other people's problems and their troubles and things like that . . . especially when you're going through hard times yourself and you're not too happy and there's no one you actually can turn to . . .

(*She puts on another mask. There is another dead silence*)

LUKE Margaret . . . you know, you really appeal to me. In many ways you do, Margaret. I kinda got it for you now: I'm sure of it . . . and it makes me feel very good. But I want you to listen to me, and please don't say anything until I'm all through. But do you know what? My life's been full of surprises, but mostly bad surprises. When I was a kid I was playing football once and I fell when some guy tackled me, I fell right straight down on a dirty piece of old glass from a broken Royal Crown Cola bottle. It cut right into my knee, clear through it went until it hit the bone, my knee bone. It happened when I was only in the sixth grade, and my mother and father then, they were pretty old-fashioned, and so they sorta took care of the cut themselves. And I was glad they did, too, because I was scared stiff, but I was even more scared of doctors and hospitals. Well, I ended up in the hospital anyway. For over a year I was laid up in bed with my right leg up in the air because poison set in. And at first it went down to my right foot, and they had to keep a big long needle stuck clear through my ankle, sticking out both ends of it, so that my leg wouldn't stop growing because, like I told you before, I was only in the sixth grade and so I was still a growing boy. But none of it worked. My leg stopped growing: my whole right leg. (*He puts another mask on; then he takes off his right shoe and begins to limp about the room; the candle flickers wildly*) You see! I got a special right shoe with a great big lift built into the bottom of it. (*He shows her*) You see! And then the poisonous gangrene—that awful green stuff, the awful rotten poison in my body—it went running through my system, the whole right side of my system until it got all the way up to my shoulder and so they had to cut away up there, here, the doctors dug deep into my right shoulder four different times so that I wouldn't die. You should see it, Margaret. You should see how ugly my right shoul-

der looks: full of gashes and holes and deep scars. When
I finally got out of the hospital I had to begin to learn to
write with my left hand. I was kicked out of high school
in my senior year because I turned out to be the meanest
kid you ever came across in your whole life. (*He takes the
mask back off*) I went to work with my father then. I
wanted to. My father's with the Sanitation Department.
I worked for the City for the last twelve years: collecting
all the garbage, and building up my body, my muscles.
(*Laughing nostalgically*) My mother helped there a lot
too: she's such a great cook, my old lady. Because of my
father she turned into one of the best Italian cooks in the
world. Every other night in the house it was either an
Italian or an Irish supper. But on Sundays it was always
Italian for my father. Hell, I had to do it, Margaret: work
on the garbage trucks, because it was part of the family:
my father wanted it that way. If he was a lawyer, that's
what I would'uve been; if he was a barber, then I
would'uve been one too. Nothing scared me on those
bright yellow garbage trucks: the live, half-dead brown
rats that would sometimes come jumping out at me . . .
(*He laughs*) . . . and all those millions of hungry stupid
running cockroaches! None of it ever bothered me. I got
used to it fast. I'm not afraid of anything. You know,
Margaret . . . you know, I have never slept with a
woman in my whole life! You can't believe that, can you?
I never did, though, and that's the honest to God truth,
Margaret. I was afraid, you know what I mean? I was
scared and I was so ashamed. Ashamed of this limp; my
short right leg. (*He begins to hobble around the room
again*) Ashamed of my scar on my right weak knee.
Ashamed of my shoulder: the ugliest right shoulder you
ever saw in your whole life! I couldn't hold a girl in my
arms with this shoulder, you know what I'm saying,
Margaret? I had a couple of bad surprises with a couple
of different girls, right when we were ready to finally go

to bed together. I HATED WHAT HAPPENED! And before I knew it I was running. I ran so fast after that! I ran a thousand miles after that! (*A pause*) Do you know why I finally left home, why I finally quit the Sanitation Department two days ago and came here to live all by myself? Because my father caught me the other day . . . he suddenly came into my bedroom and he caught me doing it all by myself! I've been doing it all by myself ever since I can remember because I didn't feel ashamed then, by myself, alone, enjoying it without being scared of what the girl was really thinking about me. I was never so ashamed in my whole life: the way I was when my father caught me the other day. And he was really lousy about it too, really and truly lousy about it all. Yeah, Margaret Moon, wherever you go in life, it's full of surprises! But mostly bad surprises. I DON'T LIKE MYSELF! That's it! I HATE MYSELF: LUKE LOVELLO! I hate him!

> (*He sits back down on the bed and puts the mask back on. There is a long silence. They both sit there in the flickering candlelight wearing their Halloween masks*)

MARGARET (*Finally*) I'm so very sorry, Luke . . .
> (MARGARET *takes off her mask. Then* LUKE *takes off his*)

LUKE (*After a long pause*) You look real good. You have a beautiful face. You got lips like a couple of ripe red plums. You know why I said plums instead of cherries? Because I got this good feeling going on inside of me that you're different than most women I've ever known. I like your eyes most of all, Margaret Moon . . . (MARGARET *smiles at him.* LUKE *gets up from the bed and goes to her. He kneels down before her. He touches her ankles*) You got nice ankles, too. (MARGARET *puts her hand on his head.* LUKE *stiffens a little. Then she begins to run her fingers through his hair. He begins to get nervous. He jumps up and quickly places his right hand on one of her breasts; then he pulls it away fast*) You see, I'm scared! Even with you. I'm scared . . . afraid. I don't know what to do. Look . . . I . . . maybe . . . if I can find . . . but they stole it! I mean, *no,* they didn't steal it! I must have left it in the bathroom: the . . . little solid-gold box with the diamond on top of it. My uncle who works in Las Vegas, he's tall, dark, and handsome, he hires the beautiful tall showgirls for the famous night-clubs there . . . my uncle, he gave me the fancy little box to keep them in. "A man should always carry his . . . safeties . . . with him," he told me. Excuse me a minute, Margaret. I'll go into the bathroom to see if they're there. (LUKE *goes to the door and opens it. He exits into the hallway and then disappears into the bathroom.* MARGARET *finally gets up. She stands staring at the opened door. Suddenly she runs, slams it shut, and then locks it.* LUKE *comes running out of the bathroom*) I can't seem to find my little rubber box made of solid gold with the diamond on top of it. (*He tries to open the door*) Hey, Margaret, you locked the door! Hey, open it up, will you? Hey, do you hear me? (*He waits for a minute.* MARGARET *stands still*) Hey Margaret, why did you do that? Awwwwww . . . c'mon! What are you doing to me? (*He begins to bang on the door*) C'mon, open it up! Will you please? Will you please open it up? (*He is almost on the verge of tears*) I don't deserve this! How come? Did I scare you? Did my limp make you sick? Did my story about my scars and gashes and limp and everything make you sick? Please don't say that it did! Please don't! I know! It was because I was too forward with you, wasn't it? That's it! I was too fresh with you, that's it, isn't it? That's why you're mad and why you won't open the door, isn't it? Because I touched your ankle, and because I touched . . . your breast. I'm sorry, Margaret Moon, I really am. (*He begins to rap on the door again; then he stops and waits. There is finally a long pause, a strange silence.* LUKE's *manner is very positive*) Margaret, you can't do this to me! I want you . . . and I know that you want me. I know that it will be all right. It won't be like it was with the other girls. (*A pause*) Margaret, it won't be that way with you. I can tell . . . I swear to God . . . please, Margaret Moon?

 (*Another moment passes.* MARGARET *goes to the window and opens it. Music is heard blaring in: Spanish-type music: a romantic mambo perhaps, with a marvelous rhythm to it. She finally goes to the door and unlocks it; she moves back into the middle of the room, waiting.* LUKE *smiles a bit. He pushes the door gently open and then he enters the room. He stops and stares at her; his smile goes away. He turns and closes the door behind him. He picks up a mask and puts it on. Then he picks up a mask for* MARGARET. *He begins to limp toward her. She goes to meet him, takes the mask he hands her, and then she drops it to the floor. She removes his mask from his face. She slowly puts her hands up to his face. They stare at one another in a half-embrace. There is a slow fadeout*)

Curtain

Ferryboat

FERRYBOAT *was presented by Theatre Genesis on September 2, 1965, at St. Mark's Church in-the-Bowery, New York City, with the following cast:*

(*In order of appearance*)

THE GIRL Stephanie Gordon
JOEY   Kevin O'Connor

Directed by Ralph Cook

THE PEOPLE OF THE PLAY

JOEY, 28, and good-looking. He wears a white-on-white dress shirt, a plain light-blue silk necktie, a neatly cut midnight-blue suit, and perfectly shined black shoes. His topcoat is also midnight blue. He wears a flashy gold wrist watch, a sparkling ring, and a tie clip and cuff links that match.

THE GIRL, about 19 or 20, and really quite beautiful. She has long black hair, a snow-white face devoid of any makeup, and a very fine figure. She wears a slightly wrinkled, lightly soiled woman's trenchcoat, black high-heels, and no stockings.

WHERE THEY ARE

Aboard the Staten Island Ferry.

The sound of a foghorn blowing in the darkness of the theatre; the whistle of a ferryboat; fading in: churning sounds of the ferryboat on the moving waters of the bay.

As the lights slowly come up we hear the faint cries of sea gulls in the distance. We are in the ferryboat interior: a particular section of it. THE GIRL *appears. She is pleased, or so it seems, at having found a remote area in which to be by herself. She sits down on one of the passengers' benches, facing the audience. She makes herself comfortable and then begins to read a book.*

Eventually, JOEY *enters through the audience. It is obvious that he has been watching* THE GIRL. *He is sipping coffee from a paper container and holds a doughnut. He gives the place a good "going-over" and then* THE GIRL *becomes irresistible to him.*

JOEY   You don't mind, do you, miss?

GIRL   Mind what?

JOEY   If I sit here next to you, I mean.
(*He sits*)

GIRL   You already are, aren't you?

JOEY   Yeah, I guess I am. (*He laughs*) Well, no matter, miss, thanks anyway . . . (*He sips*) Hey, how about some of this coffee? It's a regular one . . . milk and sugar. Is that the way you take it?

GIRL   (*Icily*)   Only black.

JOEY Let me buy you one then, okay? (THE GIRL *gives out with an impatient sigh and goes back to her book*) That book sure has you interested, doesn't it?

GIRL (*Without looking up*) You're absolutely right.

JOEY You sure you don't want a coffee?

GIRL Positively!

JOEY It's the best thing they sell . . . the coffee on this ferryboat . . . it's good . . . always fresh, too, that's the reason why. But it's only natural that it should be. Big turnover. They have to keep making it all of the time. You know . . . like the automat . . . food's always fresh there, too, because of the big turnover. (*Sipping some more*) Wow! Hot! But good! Darn good! You sure you don't want a coffee? (*A moment of silence*) I'm buying. A black coffee, okay? You said you take it black. (*Another moment of silence*) Boy, just look at you, will you. Your eyes haven't blinked since we started talking to each other. You're certainly a concentrator, aren't you? It must be a good story that you're reading. (*Unwrapping the doughnut*) Here. How about this? The doughnuts are always fresh here, too. You know . . . the big turnover, and all that . . . like the automat. Would you like half of it? It's a plain one. No sugar, no cinnamon, no chocolate. Who needs all that junk, right? Especially a woman . . . a woman like you . . . no makeup, nothing fancy, just a pure-type beauty, that's all. A natural. (*More silence*) You don't want any, huh? Well, okay. (*He begins to chew*) Really tasty, this plain doughnut. (*He sips*) This fresh coffee . . . delicious. (*He takes another bite from the doughnut*) You know, miss . . . when I first walked in here, and I spotted you, well, I said to myself, I know that broad, I mean, girl, *woman*, from somewheres. You looked real familiar to me. Did you ever go to high school over in Saint George? (*No response*) You didn't, huh? That's where I live, in Saint George. Went to high school there. I was born and raised on Staten Island. Still live there, too. (*He pauses*) Aw, that couldn't be right, anyway. We couldn't have gone to high school together. You must be about nineteen, twenty at the most. But not more than that, right?

GIRL (*Still reading*)   Right.

JOEY   I'm twenty-eight, myself.

GIRL (*Yawning*)   Really?

JOEY   Yeah. Long time ago. But seems like only yesterday. After I graduated from high school I took a Greyhound bus all the way out to the coast . . . L.A., Hollywood. I wanted to crash the movies. Be big-time . . . you know? Not just ordinary like everyone else. (*He sips more of the coffee*) But it was a lot tougher than I thought it would be. (*Finishing the doughnut*) I guess it was my fault, too, in a way. Too many beautiful women riding and speeding over all the streets and avenues and boulevards of ole' Hollywood. In streamlined convertibles at the flashy drive-ins and the classy motels, on the beaches and the super-duper highways, and around all kinds of all sorts of different-shaped swimming pools. It was just too much, let me tell you! I must'uve wasted an awful lot of time. You know, I should'uve been born a concentrator, like you, a concentrator. I didn't have any patience, though. Better yet, I suppose you could say that I didn't have too much control. Like, for instance, to prove my point to you, miss: I was voted the Class Wolf of my graduating class in high school in Saint George. You see what I mean? And so, when you really think about it, Hollywood was the last place I should'uve gone to. Anyway, I wasn't gettin' anywhere there, and so I got pretty disgusted after a while, with myself and with everything else out there, the people, the phonies, just everybody! And so here I am . . . I came back . . . *to here.*

GIRL (*Coldly*) Yes . . . *I know.*

JOEY But I'm learning to have more control now. (*He pauses*) Do you know what I think, though? I think the main reason why I hated Hollywood so much was because . . . well, there didn't seem to be any . . . *love* . . . there. I know that must sound pretty dumb to you because we all realize that there is love no matter where you go. Wherever there are people there is love. But, Jesus, I don't know, miss, but I felt that no one really cared about anyone else in Hollywood. To be honest with you, it scared me just a little too much. I had to come back East. (*He stares at her for a moment, awaiting any sort of reaction; she goes on reading*) Hey, miss! (*He snaps his fingers and gets up*) A frank! How about a frank? (*No answer*) Would you like a frank with sauerkraut and mustard? Or would you like one with relish and mustard? Or the whole works? That's even better still: the whole works! Why not live it up a little, huh? Go all the way! You see, they got good franks here, too. Always fresh. You know they have to be since they got such a big . . .

GIRL . . . *turnover!*
     (*There is an uneasy pause*)

JOEY (*Quietly now*) Yeah, that's it. (*A pause*) You sure you don't want one?

GIRL Positive. But why don't you go and have one?

JOEY (*Sitting back down*) Aw, not me. I eat too much sometimes. Once I was so full of tension, worrying about my future and everything, that I ended up eating five of them before the ferry even pulled in. (*A pause*) Nerves,

I guess. (*He takes out his cigarettes*) Cigarettes. I smoke a lot too, but it's not half so bad as it was before. I was really a chain-smoker once. (*Pause*) Hey, you wanna go out on deck with me? Look, it's the Statue of Liberty. Beautiful at this hour, all lit up and everything, and with the moon helping out there a lot, too. I'll bet I've seen the Statue of Liberty a million times, and I still never get tired of it. Always gives me a few butterflies in my stomach. C'mon, you wanna . . . ?

GIRL (*Cuttingly*) Noooooooo!

JOEY Oh? Well . . . you wanna come downstairs and have a smoke with me . . . on the lower deck? You can't smoke up here. (*No response*) I'm taking it for granted that you smoke. Most women I know nowadays smoke.

GIRL (*Impatiently*) You don't *know* me.
    (THE GIRL *closes her book noisily and reaches for a magazine which she accidentally drops to the floor*)

JOEY (*Quickly*) Oh, your magazine fell. Here, let me get it for you.

GIRL Thanks.

JOEY That's one of those magazines for people with intellects. Some good stories in there, too. I remember once when I was in the Air Borne over in Korea. I read a story in there because I found the magazine lying around and there was nothing else to do and so I read it. I'm not much of a reader, but I can still remember what the story was all about. It was about this guy who didn't know what he wanted to do with his life. He was, well, he was *searching!* You understand, miss? *Searching* . . . he really felt, deep down inside of him, this guy in the story, that he wanted to be big-time . . . you know, the way I wanted to be big-time, and so I took off for Hollywood . . .

well, this guy in the story felt the need to do cultured-type things; he had very artistic ideas about himself and about life in general. (*A pause*) But he only thought about it all; he really never tried to do any of them. Now, if I remember right, the main reason he didn't try to do any of them was because he knew that he had to get a good job and make some money . . . real fast . . . for sharp clothes and a neat car, and things like that. I can't remember . . . how the story ended up . . . but I do remember that it was pretty sad. (*A pause*) Well, anyway, I wish I could figure out who you remind me of. (*A sudden sigh*) Oh, now wait a minute! Wait just one minute! I got it! I know! (*He snaps his fingers triumphantly in mid-air*) Elizabeth Taylor!

 (*There is a brief pause*)

GIRL (*Very faintly*) Oh . . . ?

JOEY Ah! I finally got a smile out of you . . . not a very big one . . . but still, it's a smile anyway. (*More confident than ever now*) Yep . . . Elizabeth Taylor . . . what a face that woman has! (*He makes comfortable, relaxing sounds*) No makeup, either. She doesn't need any. Like you, miss . . . one of those real true beauties. I mean now, for instance, you don't need anything to help you—no tricks. Just look at you: nothing fancy at all: a plain trenchcoat, no stockings. You don't need any gimmicks because you got a face like a wild dream, baby. You know what you remind me of? (*No answer*) You remind me of one of those classical pieces of fine Greek sculpture. And you know something else? You look even better than Elizabeth Taylor. I suppose that's because you're so much younger. You've got everything in your favor. (*He begins to whistle softly*) Is it annoying you, miss?

GIRL Is *what* annoying me?

JOEY   My whistling. Since you're trying to read. I'll stop if you want me to.

GIRL   It's not that bad.

JOEY   You mean you're saying I'm a good whistler?

GIRL   I suppose so.

JOEY   Thanks. You know, you should see me on the dance floor.

GIRL   Do you whistle when you dance, too?

JOEY   Come to think of it now, you'd be a big hit at Roseland. You ever been there?

GIRL   Been where?

JOEY   To Roseland.

GIRL   I never heard of it.

JOEY   Well, I go there a lot, being a good dancer and everything. You'd be the main attraction because you're such a true beauty. What I mean to say is, some of the girls there, they'd probably be true-looking beauties too, if they didn't wear so much makeup. (*He sighs*) It's the same at work. I'm the manager of a five-and-ten . . . one of the biggest and newest in New York. Great location. Some people say it's the best one around. Very good chances for advancing myself. From manager on upward! Who knows, huh? It's the five-and-ten in the new Socony-Mobil Building. You know the one: all made of bright aluminum, very modern. The first aluminum building ever built. It's right across the street from the Chrysler Building. Now there's a building for you! The Chrysler Building! I don't know what all the fuss is over the Empire State Building. It's just taller, that's all. But I think the Chrysler Building is beautiful. Did you ever look up at it on a clear afternoon when the sky is bright blue and the sun is shining? Well, it almost looks as though it were painted against the sky. I never saw anything so great and tall; that perfect-looking spire with that tremendous needle point going way up there in the painted blue. I swear to God, it's like a huge modern painting. Anyway, the girls there . . . the ones who work for me at the five-and-ten where I'm the manager . . . all of them, trying just too hard to look too good. They don't need all that stuff on their faces. But I get along with them okay. I'm a good boss to work for. Ask any of 'em, they'll tell you. Of course, I could tell them to do anything, and they'd do it, too. Most of them, well, you know how it is . . . young boss, bachelor, and everything . . . they all sort of got eyes for me. But it's all right I guess; I even let them call me by my first name, Joey. Except when the district manager is on the scene. Then they have to call me Mr. Dove. That's my name, by the way, Joey Dove. What's yours?

GIRL (*After a pause*)   It's not important.

JOEY (*Uneasily*)   Well, anyway . . . that's the way it goes, huh? (*A depressed tone*) Pretty warm in here, don't you think? (*No response*) I think I'll take off my coat . . . unload some of the pressing weight. (*He removes his topcoat*) Whenever I get . . . *depressed,* I usually begin to perspire. I get very warm and full of tension. Not a cool tension like most people, but a warm tension. I'm a funny guy, you know? Everyone thinks I'm a happy-go-lucky person with no troubles at all. But if they only knew about how . . . *sad* . . . I can get sometimes. I guess I think too much; maybe I'm alone more than I should be. (*Chuckling*) Lone wolves . . . loners like myself: I wonder if they all think . . . (*Laughing loudly now*) about suicide the way I do. But naturally it doesn't mean a thing. I've been interested in that subject

ever since I can remember. What about you? You seem
to be a loner. Do you ever think about committing suicide? (*No answer*) Really warm in here.

GIRL   Why don't you go out on deck? It's always *cool* out
there.

JOEY   Sometimes . . . *too* cool. Well . . . what about
it?

GIRL   What about what?

JOEY   Coming out on deck with me?

GIRL   No, thanks.

JOEY   Aw, c'mon. Besides, we'll be docking any minute
now.

GIRL   I'm fine the way I am.

JOEY   I always get a big kick out of when we're pulling in
on these ferries. All the bumps and the noise . . . and
the crazy white foam that the water makes! C'mon . . .
(THE GIRL *fumbles nervously with the magazine; she is
unsure*) You're going to wear that magazine out.

GIRL   It's my business.

JOEY (*Quickly*)   Do you like to dance?

GIRL   Never!

JOEY   Not at all, huh? That's a real shame. What I mean to
say is, I think dancing is the best medicine for anything.
Everyone should like it . . . should know how to dance.
It's good for the . . . *ego*, I guess. Yeah, that's it . . .
the perfect medicine for everybody's ego. It makes you
feel free and easy . . . keeps people young and even a
little wild. The best way possible, too, for men and

women to meet each other, to get acquainted easier. (*He hesitates to get a reaction, then continues*) You should take it up sometimes. You don't know what you're missing. I've won a few dance contests. Last year, over at Palisades Park, across the Hudson River, I won for doing the frug. About a month ago I got fifty dollars, first prize, this girl and me, for doing the bossa nova like two professionals. It was up at Freedomland in the Moon Bowl. Ever been there? The Moon Bowl's my favorite spot for dancing. It's really okay. Listen, miss . . . maybe you'd like to go with me this Saturday night?

GIRL (*To herself*)   Oh, dear . . .
       (*A short pause*)

JOEY   You didn't answer me, miss. Dancing? How about it? I think you'd . . .

GIRL (*Cutting in, sharply*)   *No,* thank you!

JOEY (*Trying to show no concern over her attitude*)   They always have a big-name singer, and there's always a top-name band for dancing. (*For the first time his voice sounds tense*) You sure you don't want to go sometimes?

GIRL (*Tiredly, with a sigh*)   Thank you . . . but I told you—no.

JOEY (*Becoming uneasy*)   Well, anyway, the girls at work . . . I mean, the ones who work for me . . . and the babes at Roseland . . . they all find me a pretty attractive guy . . . no matter what you think, miss. I had a heck of a time when I was in high school. One heck of a time, let me tell you! The babes never left me alone. I think that's why I went to Hollywood. I knew I had what it takes. My old man was real proud of me. He used to call me Broadway Joe. He called me it all the way up until the time my mother died; then he lost practically all of his humor after that. He passed away almost exactly a year to the very day that she died—my mother. (*He pauses*) You know, I'll bet you have a hard time, too, don't you, miss? I mean, with that face of yours, like a beautiful piece of fine Greek sculpture . . . it's real classical-looking.

(*A brief pause*)

GIRL (*Then, firmly*)   You know something? (*She looks straight at him now*)

JOEY   What? (*THE GIRL gets up and begins stuffing her magazines and her books into her large pocketbook*)

GIRL (*Very clearly*)   If you like the crazy white foam that the water makes so much, then why don't you try jumping into it sometime? (*THE GIRL turns to move away from JOEY, but he pulls her instantly by the arm, and then he holds her still and with great firmness. THE GIRL remains there, almost motionless, simply staring at him. There is the indication of a very slight smile on her lips*)

JOEY (*Finally*)   Yeah . . . miss . . . ! (*His voice is on the brink of cracking*) Yeah . . . ! I may just do that some time . . . I may just give it a try! (*They stop and stare at each other. JOEY keeps a tight grip on her arm. Then he begins to shake it lightly up and down*) All I wanted, miss . . . all I want now . . . is to . . . *fuck you* . . . YEAH! (*He glances quickly around them*) How about that now? Do you like that kind of language, huh? Yeah, yeah: I guess you kinda do. You're that different type of girl. I don't ever meet them much: real modern, huh? Maybe, maybe, I should have just said that to you in the first place, right? That's all I want: to get to fuck you. I've made a fool of myself, haven't I?

Talking and talking , a mile a minute. About myself, about everything . . . and all because I just wanted to get to fuck you . . . *do you understand?*

GIRL (*After a moment*)   I . . . I . . . where are you going?

JOEY   Shut up for a minute! (*He eases his grip on her arm*) I'm lonely, baby, but you're even lonelier . . . you sat there, miss, you sat there, and you listened to everything I said. You never made even one try at getting away from me, did you?
      (THE GIRL *doesn't reply. We hear the roar of the waves outside and of the ferryboat pulling in at the docks, hitting and splashing against the great wooden barriers*)

GIRL (*After a long moment*)   Where are you going . . . in Saint George, that is?
      (JOEY *begins to smile a little*)

JOEY   I live alone. On Chapin Avenue.

GIRL   I know where it is.

JOEY   C'mon. Let's go out on deck. Let's go out and look at the crazy white foam that the water makes . . . (*He takes her by the arm as she steps down off the edge of the stage*) What do you do? Better yet: what's your name?
      (THE GIRL *stops and turns to face him*)

GIRL   My name is Eleanor. I go to school—college—majoring in English Literature . . . (*The lights begin to fade*) minoring in philosophy . . . and the Social Patterns of Urban Love . . . Sarah Lawrence . . .
      (*She turns and begins to walk through the audience*)

JOEY   I thought you said it was Eleanor . . .
(*He follows after her. The lights are fully out now. We hear the rumbling of the ferryboat and the splashing of the water, and the rocking of the creaking wooden beams. Then there are just the cries of sea gulls announcing the arrival of the ferryboat*)

The Shirt   Curtain

THE SHIRT *was presented by The Eugene O'Neill Memorial Theatre Foundation in Waterford, Connecticut, in July, 1966, as a staged reading, with the following cast:*

(*In order of appearance*)

CLARENCE   Eugene O'Connell
TWILA   Beth Turner
MARCEY   Tom Mook

Directed by Melvin Bernhardt

THE PEOPLE OF THE PLAY

(They are all in their 20's)

CLARENCE,   a Southern gentleman. At first he speaks with a disarming Southern accent in an intelligent tone of voice. When he puts on the shirt, there is an immediate transformation: semi-Southern, semi-illiterate, semi-hillbilly.

TWILA,   a lovely Negro girl.

MARCEY,   a good-looking New York boy.

WHERE THEY ARE

A room of a cheap hotel in the Times Square area of Manhattan, during the early nighttime.

When the curtain goes up we are in a darkened hotel room. A blinking neon sign outside one of the two windows makes an eerie setting of flashing red and green. Both windows are partly opened, and the worn and flimsy curtains are waving lightly from an early night breeze outside.

There are occasional sounds of automobile horns: muffled and lonely. Then, fire sirens are heard zooming fast on the streets far below: faint and perhaps foreboding.

Music is coming from somewhere: two or three different kinds of music mingling all at once in the air. There is a soft sound of shattering glass from somewhere, and of a door slamming shut. Then, voices are heard in the distance: vague and incoherent at first. They slowly grow closer to us.

TWILA *is heard giggling quietly.*

MARCEY'S VOICE   Kiss me . . .

TWILA'S VOICE   It wouldn't be polite . . .

MARCEY'S VOICE   I want to kiss you because I love you. How can that not be polite?

TWILA'S VOICE   It's just not nice in front of him—our new friend.

CLARENCE'S VOICE   I don't mind a bit. I invited you two lovebirds up to my room because I wanted to enjoy myself, and because I wanted the two of you to enjoy yourselves.

(*A key is heard being turned in a lock.* TWILA *giggles again*)

MARCEY'S VOICE   Twila-baby: you're drunk . . .
(TWILA *laughs quietly.* MARCEY *joins in.* CLARENCE *is now laughing with them. The door of the room swings open; the ceiling lights are switched on.* CLARENCE *enters first, followed by* TWILA *and* MARCEY)

CLARENCE   This is it, children. Welcome, and make yourselves at home.

MARCEY (*Looking around*) Jesus . . . I mean, but Jesus . . . !

CLARENCE   Is there something wrong?

MARCEY   We gotta get you a nicer place than this. I mean, man, you deserve a nicer place than this.

CLARENCE   Oh?

TWILA   Stop it, Marcey . . .

CLARENCE   Maybe we should go back downstairs . . . ?

MARCEY   Anywhere but here.

TWILA   No, of course not. I like it here. Don't you pay attention to Marcey. He simply doesn't think when he's been drinking. It would be nice if you apologized, Marcey.

MARCEY   I didn't do anything.

TWILA   You were only rude, that's all.

MARCEY   I was?

TWILA   Terrible . . .

CLARENCE   He was honest. That's what matters.

TWILA   He was rude.

CLARENCE   But I don't mind because he's right.

TWILA   I disagree.

MARCEY   You're drunk, baby. I mean now: just look at you.

TWILA   That's not true. I only had two drinks.

MARCEY   You had three. And that's enough for you. Three dry martinis. That's plenty for my little baby.

TWILA   You're treating me like a child again.

MARCEY   You are a child. A beautiful bruised child.

TWILA   Oh, stop it. You're drunk too. I can tell, when you begin talking like that.

CLARENCE   He sounds like a poet talking. I like it.

MARCEY   Thatta boy, Clarence.

TWILA   I like this room a lot.

MARCEY   I think it's depressing.

TWILA   Marcey, you're terrible . . .

CLARENCE   But I suppose he's right, young lady. You Northern people are progressive souls. You have more sophistication. I can understand why this place, this room, would give an unpleasant impression. I know all about you children: young ladies and young gentlemen of the liberal northlands. Aw, c'mon in, c'mon in. Once I get started talking I forget to ever shut up.

TWILA (*Smiling*)   But we already are in . . .

CLARENCE   No, not until the door is shut: that's when you are in, all nice and secure and cozy . . .

TWILA   Oh?
  (CLARENCE *closes the door gently*)

CLARENCE   There, you see? And I'm sorry. I must apologize to the both of you, talking the way I just was, saying things that really aren't too profound, and then you friendly people simply listening to me in order to be polite . . .

MARCEY   There's nothing to be sorry about, man, nothing.

TWILA   Marcey is right.
  (CLARENCE *turns on the table lamps*)

CLARENCE   That's a lot better, don't you think? Comfortable lighting . . . and, of course, comfortable people. Sit down now, go on, the two of you, sit down and relax and take it nice and easy. (*He takes off his jacket*) And they all shoot their mouths off about Southern hospitality, down where I come from. If they only knew how kind and friendly you Northern folks are. Then they wouldn't be half so conceited. I have been in this great metropolis, this fine and hospitable city now, for only three days and three nights, and do you people know: I almost hate the idea of going back down to where I come from. Never before did I ever believe that the day would come when I would begin to feel a little disliking for the town and the state that I was born and raised in. C'mon now—take off your coats and make yourselves at home, and then I'll make us all a nice drink.

MARCEY   Like a mint julep, maybe?

TWILA   I love the taste of mint.

MARCEY (*Singing, jokingly*) "One mint julep . . . da, da, da!"

(MARCEY *tries to dance a mambo with* TWILA)

TWILA Marcey, you're drunk. You never want to dance unless you're drunk . . .

MARCEY Not as drunk as you . . .

CLARENCE You know, the main reason why I asked you two lovebirds up here in the first place was because you are both just brimming over with humor; good, innocent people with such bright and cheerful outlooks on life in general. I'm leaving in the morning and I couldn't think of a better way to spend my last night here. (CLARENCE *goes to the night table and opens the drawer. He takes out a pint bottle*) Here it is. A little bottle of it, filled to the top, and unopened, for the three of us to share . . . and share alike. Cognac. Pure French cognac.

MARCEY You got taste, Clarence.

TWILA I love cognac.

CLARENCE That's very good to hear.

MARCEY And I'll tell you what, Clarence. After we kill the cognac, we'll leave here and have a good time in some other place. The drinks will be on me then . . .

TWILA And me . . .

CLARENCE A proper lady should never have to pay. Especially for a gentleman. I can always help out, Marcey, in case you run out of money. I still have a few extra dollars left.

(CLARENCE *begins to look around the room*)

TWILA Thank you, Clarence.

CLARENCE   I got two glasses and a paper cup. I hope you don't mind. I'll drink out of the paper cup if it's all right with the two of you.

MARCEY   I'll drink out of the paper cup.

CLARENCE   It wouldn't be proper.

MARCEY   Yes it would.

CLARENCE   But you're my guest.
      (*By now* CLARENCE *has poured out the cognac. He hands the half-filled glasses to* TWILA *and* MARCEY; *he takes the paper cup*)

TWILA   Thank you.

MARCEY   Yes, thanks.

CLARENCE   You're both welcome.

MARCEY   A toast then!

TWILA   Yes, a toast to Clarence!
      (TWILA *and* MARCEY *raise their glasses high;* CLARENCE *does so too*)

CLARENCE   I think we should drink to you two lovebirds.

MARCEY   To Clarence!

TWILA   Clarence!
      (CLARENCE *smiles. They all drink together*)

CLARENCE   Nice warm stuff . . .
      (*There is a brief odd silence; they all sort of half-smile at one another*)

TWILA (*Finally*)   I think we should all sit.

CLARENCE   Oh, yes, by all means. (CLARENCE *goes to the only comfortable-looking chair in the room and fluffs up the cushions a bit for* TWILA *to sit in. He motions to* TWILA) For you, young lady.

TWILA   Thank you. (*She sits*) Do you know something? I could do a lot for this place. I could make it into a lovely little room for cozy living.

MARCEY (*Sitting on the edge of the bed*)   Oh, Jesus, there she goes: interior decorating again.

CLARENCE (*Sitting in a straight wooden desk chair in the center of the room*)   That's right, Twila. It's your line of work: that interior decorating sort of business, isn't it?

TWILA   When I finish the school I'll really be ready. I can hardly wait. I want to paint, but I don't think I can. I'm afraid I'd be terrible at it. Maybe in a few years from now, when I'm older. Meanwhile, interior decorating will be fine for me. It's creative in its own special way.

MARCEY   And the money, honey. The money you'll make. It's a racket. You can make an awful lot of money, honey.

CLARENCE   What would you do, Twila?

TWILA   What do you mean?

CLARENCE   I mean if you had the chance to do this place all over again from scratch.

TWILA (*Taking a long sip*)   Well, I'd . . .
         (*She begins to cough*)

MARCEY (*After finishing a long sip*)   Honey, you're going to get sick.
         (TWILA *continues to cough.* CLARENCE *goes to her*)

TWILA (*Coughing*)   I can't catch my breath!

CLARENCE   Can I . . . ? Can . . . I pat your back? It will help you. I know exactly how to do it.
(TWILA *motions for him to go ahead. He does so.*)

MARCEY (*Getting up*)   You okay, honey?

CLARENCE   Is everything all right now?

TWILA (*Her coughing has gone*)   I'm fine now . . .

MARCEY   You drink too fast, honey.

TWILA   Thank you, Clarence.

CLARENCE   Not at all.

MARCEY   Did you hear what I said, honey? You drink too fast.

TWILA   I don't think it's that at all. I think it's simply a matter of mixing gin with cognac. Once I get adjusted there won't be a thing to worry about.

CLARENCE   But you are all right now?

TWILA   I'm wonderful. Feeling a little high and simply wonderful.

MARCEY   Me too.

CLARENCE   So am I, then.

TWILA   Clarence, you've got to come with us tonight. A little party around the city of New York.

MARCEY   Right! When the cognac goes, then we go, the three of us.

CLARENCE   Well, I hate to butt in on you two lovebirds. Heck, you don't want me around. That old saying about "three's a crowd" might prove to be correct if I'm in the picture, and well, I wouldn't want to go back home feeling I ruined the party.

MARCEY Never!

TWILA I second that!

CLARENCE I really and truly don't know what I'm going to do with the two of you.

MARCEY Just get high with us, that's all.

TWILA It's as simple as that.

CLARENCE You people, Twila and Marcey, are certainly generous. It makes me warm all over when I hear you both talk like this. It also proves that I was right. My parents, my other relatives, my friends, they all warned me ahead of time. They said I was going to come across primarily cold people all living together in one huge cold canyon—that canyon, of course, being your exceptional city of New York—and their ideas have all been immensely inaccurate. You people are warm and your city is warm, and all my friends and relatives back down there—they're all warm, too—but it's their ideas, their everyday thoughts about what prevails up here in the benevolent North, it's their ideas that are cold, cold because they are frozen over solid without any real knowledge of the situation at hand.

MARCEY Clarence, pour yourself another drink of that pure French cognac!
       (TWILA *laughs*)

CLARENCE Thank you. I believe that I will. Now, Twila, why don't you sit down there on the bed next to your Northern gentleman escort. You see, I have my camera with me, and so I would like to take your picture together, if you both wouldn't mind. As a souvenir. As something I can go back to and look at whenever I want to recall past and pleasant memories. Is that all right with you, miss?

TWILA   I'd love to do it.
(*She sits down next to* MARCEY)

MARCEY   What about you, man? We got to have a picture of you, too.

TWILA   I'll take it—the picture of you, Clarence.

CLARENCE   Don't think about me. We . . . the three of us, we . . . I mean the two of you: you won't ever be seeing me again after tonight. So forget about me. I don't believe I'd be as happy a memory as the two of you are going to be. Now, c'mon, the two of you, take off your coats and I'll get my camera ready here.
(*The three of them all have removed their coats by now*)

TWILA   Could I have just a wee bit more of your cognac, Clarence?

CLARENCE   Why, of course.

MARCEY   You're drunk, honey.

TWILA   So are you.
(CLARENCE *pours more into their glasses*)

CLARENCE   It's for all of us to drink . . . and to get drunk . . . a nice cozy happy-go-lucky drunk.

TWILA   I believe that I would do this room in light blue. A very *deep* light blue!

MARCEY   Light blue can't be very *deep*, baby.

TWILA   I would do it deep blue like the deep blue sea. You know why? Because, and you won't believe this, but I have never seen the sea. That sounds horrible. I've never seen the ocean. Only pictures of it. I would design the curtains to look like little-girl curtains, and they would be in pure white with soft pink bows. And I would . . .

MARCEY   You're really not making much sense, baby.

TWILA   I think I am.

CLARENCE   I'm ready.

TWILA   For what?

CLARENCE   The picture-taking.

TWILA   Oh, yes, I'm sorry, of course.
(CLARENCE *clicks a picture*)

CLARENCE   There, you see. Now just a few more, okay?

TWILA   Anything you say.

MARCEY   You're drinking too fast, baby.

TWILA   I'm not a little girl any more.

MARCEY   You're a big girl, then?

TWILA   Yes.

MARCEY   Then I think it's about time the big girl here got a chance to see the sea . . . I mean the ocean.

TWILA   The great big deep blue . . . ocean!

MARCEY   Tomorrow we're going to see the ocean. I am going to take you.

TWILA   That's wonderful. And Clarence will come with us.
(CLARENCE *takes another picture*)

CLARENCE   Now just a few more.

MARCEY   You will come with us tomorrow, won't you, Clarence?

CLARENCE   If you both really want me to.

TWILA   Of course!

CLARENCE   Then I'll be glad to be a part of it.
(CLARENCE *snaps another picture*)

MARCEY   You almost through?

CLARENCE   Just a few more now. You two go right ahead with your talking and drinking and having a good time and I'll be finished before you know it. (*He clicks again*) There, you see?

TWILA   I hope I come out looking good. I feel a bit drunk and I don't think I look my best when I've been drinking. I'm not used to drinking. I just began a few months ago, Clarence, and so please be patient with me.
(CLARENCE *laughs kindly*)

MARCEY   I'm immune to the stuff . . .

TWILA   I don't think you are.

MARCEY   I'm an expert at drinking. I don't really ever get drunk. I've been drinking ever since I was sixteen. Back in Detroit. Out on the Coast. Down at Fort Sam Houston. Here in New York. I can drink anything at any time.

CLARENCE   This is it. The last one. Smile now. (*He clicks the picture*) Thank you both. (*He takes a long slug of the cognac*)

TWILA   It will be gone soon.

CLARENCE   What?

MARCEY   She's talking about the cognac.

CLARENCE   We can always get more.

TWILA   You're so positive, Clarence. I love you for it.

CLARENCE   Thank you.

MARCEY (*A pause*)   I'd do this room in green. Forest green
. . . a very rich and deep forest type of green. I think it
would be perfect in that color.

TWILA   Haven't you ever been in a forest before?

MARCEY   Once or twice, maybe.

CLARENCE   I took this room because I am on a strict budget.
This short little weekend trip up here was a sudden ex-
travagance on my part, but I don't regret it one bit. No,
sir; no, ma'am. But I suppose in a way this place is a hole.
As you both can plainly see, I even left the windows
opened so I could get the smell out. Lousy old smell: an
unlikely combination of cheap deodorant and city decay.
But don't get me wrong. I told you before, I like this city
of yours an awful lot. You people got a nice town here,
and don't allow anyone to tell you differently. Down
South where I come from, well, the cities and the towns
—they are *old* with decay. Up here in the sophisticated
North the cities and the towns—they are *new* with decay.
I am fully aware, my two new lovebird friends, that there
is a kind of hope that exists up here in the big city air, because you can work with decay that is still *new*. There is
a much better chance. But when things are *old* with decay, as I told you they are down South, it is a more diffi-
cult situation . . . an almost futile predicament. You
can preserve the *new* decay, but how can you make *old*
decay become *new*? (*Nodding his head*) No, sir; no,
ma'am. Old with decay! They refer to it down there as
Tradition! Aristocracy! Lord, but that is all has-been non-

sense! Who knows? Perhaps we can hope and pray that all is not too late; perhaps we can believe with deep concern that The Good God Almighty will, in due time, bestow upon all these relatives and friends of mine, and all of their relatives and friends as well, a sudden bolt of pure enlightenment. (*He clicks the camera again*) There now, you see? I've been talking an awful lot again, but at the very same time I managed to snap another little photograph of you two people without you even noticing it. No posing, very natural. And· so, all was not in vain; something was accomplished . . . I mean, that is . . . if my little speech was in any way dull or unimportant.

TWILA   To the contrary.

MARCEY   You should write a book, Clarence. I think it would outsell all other books. Did you ever think of that before?

CLARENCE   Writing a book takes a lot of time and strong will. I suppose I'm ashamed to confess it, but talking is a whole lot easier. Now . . . just one more picture for good luck and a happy future simply full of the best and the warmest of wishes. (*He holds up the camera again*) It would be nice and proper, I do believe sincerely, if you both sort of got a little closer maybe . . . like holding hands, or something . . . like perhaps just a little sign of an embrace of some kind, indicating, maybe, that you are both lovebirds . . . if this is acceptable to the two of you?

MARCEY   On one condition. That you promise to be our guest afterward . . .

TWILA   When the cognac is gone . . .

MARCEY   That's right . . .

TWILA   Have you ever been to the Village?

CLARENCE   You mean Greenwich Village?

TWILA   Yes, Greenwich Village.

CLARENCE (*Sheepishly*)   I never got up enough nerve. You know, like I told you people before, this is my first trip up here, and during these last three days I've spent most of it right around here in this vicinity, alone. I suppose I put limitations on myself. I should try to avoid doing things like that to myself.

MARCEY   So? Will you come with us?

CLARENCE   It would be a great pleasure. Thank you both for the invitation. And now the *last*, the *final* pose? With perhaps just that little hint of intimacy I was telling you about?

TWILA   Of course.
(MARCEY *and* TWILA *oblige as* CLARENCE *snaps the picture*)

CLARENCE   And now, more drinks!

TWILA   But maybe this time I should have a little water.
(TWILA *gets up*)

CLARENCE   I'll get it for you.
(*He takes her glass*)

TWILA   Thank you.

MARCEY   Baby, maybe you should have *all* water.
(CLARENCE *exits into the bathroom*)

TWILA   That's not fair.

MARCEY   I don't want you to get sick, baby.

TWILA   But I'm feeling happy.

MARCEY You won't be for long if you get sick.
(*The curtains wave rapidly at the windows*)

TWILA It's getting chilly in here. I think I'd better put my coat back on.

MARCEY (*Calling*) Hey, Clarence! Would it be okay with you if I closed the windows? The girl friend is getting chilly.

CLARENCE (*Offstage*) By all means, please do. (*MARCEY gets up and closes both the windows. He embraces* TWILA *and then they kiss.* CLARENCE *returns at this moment. He sees them kissing. A sudden tension shows in his face. He drops the glass of water*) Whoops now! I dropped the glass of water. (*MARCEY and TWILA break away from each other*) But it didn't break. (*He laughs uneasily*) It might be a dirty old worn-out rug, but at least it saved the glass. Now you two: sit back down there together on that nice soft bed and be cozy. I am the host. Proud that you are my guests. (*MARCEY and TWILA sit back down again on the bed.* CLARENCE *goes back into the bathroom. He calls from offstage*) It's truly a fine cognac. I asked the man— the gentleman—in the liquor store for the best cognac —French cognac—in the house.
      (*He returns with a full glass of water and hands it to* TWILA)

TWILA Thank you, Clarence.

CLARENCE You're welcome, Twila.
(TWILA *drinks half the glass of water*)

TWILA This time I'll mix the cognac with the water.
(CLARENCE *pours three new drinks*)

CLARENCE There now. Everything is all ready and rosy again. Three welcome drinks for . . . three deserving people. (*He smiles*) I keep thinking that "three is a crowd." Perhaps I really . . .

MARCEY   Nothing doing, Clarence.

TWILA   You're coming out with us afterward.

CLARENCE   You people are very bright, very optimistic . . . hospitable. And now, shall we drink some more?
(*They all lift their drinks and click them together*)

MARCEY   Luck!

TWILA   Luck!

CLARENCE (*After a pause*) Lots . . . of . . . luck! (*They all drink.* CLARENCE *finishes his in one gulp*) Ahhhhh! Don't mind me. I mean, my gulping down that cognac like that. I'm not a glutton. I simply enjoy the best of everything there is . . . and in a big way. Oh, yes! It really does make me warm inside, that pure hot alcohol. (*He drinks some more. There is a silent pause. They all sip their drinks now*) I believe it's getting late.

MARCEY   Lots of time yet.

TWILA   We've got the whole night yet.

CLARENCE (*Beginning to laugh*) It's certainly a funny sight!

MARCEY   What is?

CLARENCE (*Laughing*) The two of you: it certainly is a sight of humor to behold! I really don't know which one of you looks funnier! I mean to say now: that you are both looking pretty intoxicated to me. I like it. It's comfortable to see.
(MARCEY *and* TWILA *laugh;* CLARENCE *joins them*)

TWILA   Who looks the highest?

MARCEY   Me or Twila?

CLARENCE (*After a pause*)   Excuse me a second, but do you know, it's getting late. Perhaps I have wasted too much time already. I really have been stalling, haven't I? But we are having a good time, aren't we? (*He begins to unbutton his shirt*) I must apologize for removing my shirt this way, in front of you people, but do you know how I am suddenly looking at it? Well, I see it in brand-new terms of not placing limitations on myself. (*He removes the shirt entirely. He has a fairly good build and a hairy chest. He delights in flexing his average muscles. He tosses the shirt to the floor and stands up very straight, holding his stomach, expanding his shoulders and chest*) More! Let's have more to drink! More of that French love juice! (*He laughs and drinks some more. He takes out his wallet and searches for a folded newspaper clipping. He hands it to* MARCEY) Read that, you two lovebirds. (MARCEY *and* TWILA *show signs of slight bewilderment. They read the clipping together.* CLARENCE *bends over and drags two average-sized suitcases out from underneath the bed*) What are your opinions? What do you both think of Clarence now? (*They both turn and look at him.* CLARENCE *looks up*) And that picture of me? Isn't that *some* photograph? I would be willing to bet that you haven't ever before in your whole lives seen such a perfect specimen of sexual manhood, now, have you? (CLARENCE *takes out a shirt from one of the suitcases. He slips it on but leaves it completely unbuttoned. It is a bright loud summer shirt with short sleeves. It is wildly covered with splashes of nude girls, palm trees, and orange rays of the sun. He lights himself a cigarette and then stands before the two of them, posing*) Jist like dat perfect photograph of me, huh? How do you like it, you two? Ain't it exactly like dat beautiful pitchur of me in the newspapers? Marcey? Do you know what I would

like for you to do? I would like for you to read that clipping out loud. I want to hear it read. G'wan! Start by
readin' underneath the photograph first. Go ahead now!
You begin by readin' the caption.

MARCEY I'm . . . going to need another slug of that
cognac, man, before I do anything . . .

CLARENCE Nooooooo you don't! You read first!

MARCEY It's . . . pretty wild stuff. It's you all right. But
there's a different name here.
(TWILA *begins to stir with great discomfort*)

CLARENCE Naturally the name is different, you silly Northern boy. That's my real name you see there in the newspaper. The name I was born with, I am proud to say:
Georgie Ross Jordan. Up here, in dirty ole' Yankee land,
I am known as Clarence John Bullock. It's an artificial
name I have up here . . . jist like everything else in
dirty ole' Yankee territory: fake . . . false . . . in-
awwwthentic! (CLARENCE *drags the other suitcase over
by his feet and then he sits down before the two of them.*
MARCEY *starts to get up*) No, boy! You stay there! You sit
now! And you read like I told you before. You hear me?
Hey, you know what I think? Maybe it's better if the
colored girl here read it instead. How about it, colored
girl? You wanna read it out loud?

TWILA I . . . would like to use your bathroom . . . if
you don't mind?

CLARENCE Goddam now! You're both like two nervous
little flies! (MARCY *holds* TWILA's *hand*) I'll tell you
what: you, Marcey, can have another drink of that
French cognac. And you, Twila, can use my bathroom.
But first, I wanna hear that newspaper story read to me.
Time's runnin' out, boy! . . . girl!

(*There is a long uneasy pause.* CLARENCE *smiles long
and comfortably*)

MARCEY (*Reading*)　"Georgie Ross Jordan, looking like a
beachboy in the middle of winter, is taken into custody
after being arrested for the rape of a thirteen-year-old
girl who was acting as a baby-sitter in the house next
door."

CLARENCE (*Laughing*)　Ain't that the perfect caption for
that there pitchur? Ain't it now? (*He drinks*) Okay, okay,
New York boy. G'wan! Start readin' the story itself.
(TWILA *begins to stir*) You sit still, Twila-girl! Continue,
Marcey-boy!

MARCEY (*Reading*)　"Georgie Ross Jordan, twenty-five, of
Sillsville, was arrested here tonight, Christmas Eve, at
nine-thirty, in connection with the rape of a thirteen-
year-old baby-sitter. The girl, whose name is being with-
held because of her age, was . . ."

CLARENCE (*Laughing*)　Ain't that a bitch? Ain't that a
downright goddam bitch? Believe me when I tell you
that that little blonde girl ain't never again gonna have it
as good as she did that unforgettable night: Christmas
Eve. Shiiiittt! I gave her the *biggest* and the *best* present
she'll ever get in her whole life! (*Bending over and opening the other suitcase*) Yeahhhh . . . it was jist like one
of those nice sweet-smellin' flowers . . . ohhhhh, so
much like a fresh little buttercup . . . (*He takes a small
rifle from the suitcase*) How do you like it? White boy?
. . . Colored girl? Ain't it a beauty? My best friend: my
dear little carbine rifle. (*He jiggles it in his hand*) It's
a light mother . . . (*He kisses it*) Semi-automatic . . .
thirty caliber . . . a handy mother with *perfect* fire
power! (*He leers at them*) Of course they all say that it
has limited range, but ole' Clarence John Bullock, alias

George Ross Jordan—or is it the other way around?—
anyway, I got it so's there ain't never no limitations . . .
I got it under control, this little beauty, right where I always want it. Ohhhh yes . . . it does everything I wish
for it to do. And tonight it's gonna kill you . . . (*He
points the carbine at* TWILA) And then you . . . (*He
points it to* MARCY) Or the other way 'round . . . it
don't really matter that much. (*He sits back in the chair,
the carbine in his lap, always pointing to* TWILA *and*
MARCEY) And I want for both of you dirty Yankee lovebirds to keep your mouths shut. Marcey? You're jist
gonna have to forget about that drink I was promisin'
you. There's jist enough to last me. Twila? Hey, Twila,
nigger girl! You stop that lookin' at me. You give me a
nicer look than that. And you, Marcey, I want you to
give me a nicer look than that, too. I want for you to both
be smilin' and happy again, like you all were before. Hey,
Twila, nigger girl: you pour some of that French juice in
my glass for me. G'wan! Do as I say now, black honey
. . . more of that French juice in my single paper cup!
(TWILA *begins to obey him, but* MARCEY *holds her back*)
You take your hands off her, Mr. Northern White Trash!
You hear me now? You let her be! Twila? Do as I say,
honey. (TWILA *pours the cognac for him*) That's a good
little girl. (*Chuckling*) Twila . . . what the hell kinda
name is that . . . Twila? It sounds like one of those
Indian names or somethin', don't it now? 'Course we all
know that you ain't no Indian. I understand that they're
almost all *extinct* now in this country . . . yeahhhhhh!
Twila . . . it's a good name for you, ain't it? . . . Twila,
jist like *twilight!* You gotta admit that sometimes the
niggers really have some good common sense when they
pick their names for their little colored chillun. Ain't
that right, now? 'Course whenever this here boy here—
SOUTHERN GENTLEMAN GEORGIE—whenever he
thinks of the twilight he includes the stars, too. Honey-

Twila, I don't see any white stars on you. All I can see is
the *black* night! (*He laughs*) Hey, Marcey! How are you
feelin', boy? You don't look so scared any more. You look
pretty mad now. Yes, sir, I can see how mad you are.
And you, Twila! You don't look so scared any more,
either. You're all gettin' jist as mad as your white New
York boy friend here. I don't like that too much. It ain't
gonna be too much fun if I'm gonna have to kill you people when you aren't even scared. (*He lifts the carbine
and points it directly at both of them*) It is all loaded and
all ready to perform its duties. (*He lowers it again and
rests it in his lap; he takes a swig of the cognac and then
belches*) One thing that is nice, though: you two people
are obeyin' me. You're both keepin' those Yankee tongues
quiet. Hey, Marcey? What kinda name is that? C'mon
now! You talk because I want you to talk. You hear? Hey,
boy, you listenin' to me? (*He lifts the carbine in the direction of* TWILA) I don't want you to be still like that. If
you don't answer me when I want for you to answer me,
then I get mad. You want me to blast your nigger girl
friend right now, in front of you? What kinda name is
Marcey?

MARCEY It's short for Marcello.

CLARENCE (*Lowering the carbine*) Spell it!
(MARCEY *hesitates;* TWILA *gives him a look of vague
encouragement.* CLARENCE *belches again*)

MARCEY (*Spelling*) M-A-R-C-E-L-L-O.

CLARENCE Thatta boy. It's a foreign name, ain't it?

MARCEY I don't know. You tell me.

CLARENCE What kind, boy? What kind? What nationality?

MARCEY I'm an American.

CLARENCE   That ain't no American-soundin' name to me. Are you one of those Italians?

MARCEY   That's right.

CLARENCE   Shiiiiiiittttt! You ain't really an American then. You're one of those wops, that's all you are. And you know what that means? It means you must be one of those Romans, right? Ain't you one of those Roman Catholics? G'wan, white-trash wop-boy . . . unbutton your shirt there. (MARCEY *does not respond*) I SAID . . . UNBUTTON YOUR SHIRT THERE AT THE TOP! I wanna see for sure! (MARCEY *unbuttons his shirt halfway*) Jist as I thought! You're wearin' one of those medals of the devil! You're a goddam Roman, all right. This is certainly goin' to be some killing! An extra-special killing, yes, sir! A nigger girl and a Roman wop. Yeahhh! (CLARENCE *stands up now, holding his carbine; he walks about occasionally*) I got this buddy of mine—Billy-Boy Summers—we been friends all our lives; well, when I told him I was comin' up here to Yankee-town and that I intended to shoot to kill the first mixed couple I saw, he was real happy about it, and he said to me: "If you find one of those integrated couples where the white half is also a Roman—well, boy, then you got yourself *a real prize!*" And then he said: "Of course if you find one of those mixed couples where the white part of it is a *Jew*, that's even better yet!" And then he thought for a second or two, my ole' buddy, Billy-Boy Summers, and then he said: "But 'course nowadays I'm beginnin' to think that a nigger-lovin' white Protestant is *the grandest prize* of all!" You see, you two people, my buddy Billy-Boy, he's wantin' so bad to shoot at that nigger-lovin' President we got in the *White* House. And did you know that that Lady Bird's got Spanish blood in her system? Ain't that a goddam shame? It ain't like it used to be any more. They might as well call it the *Colored* House with all those mixed-breeds runnin' around inside there like that! (*He lights himself another cigarette; he goes to a mirror and admires himself*) I always look my best in this shirt. This shirt always does things to me. I'm a different person when I put this shirt on. It's a good thing I didn't have this shirt on when I met you people downstairs in that barroom, 'cause if I was and I had this carbine with me I would'uve shot you both down dead right on the spot! That's a fact! (*Laughing*) You really walked right into my nice neat little trap, didn't you? I laid out one of those invisible Southern spiderwebs and you two never even knew about it. HA, HA! BUT NOW YOU KNOW ABOUT IT, DON'T YOU! Your city is a city of mixed-breeds. It's full of travelin' gypsies. You people aren't real true Americans. SHIT! Marcey, you come from Detroit, and your mommy and daddy are foreigners. And you, nigger girl, tellin' me you originally come from New Orleans—'course your black folks before you all came from Africa, which is pretty goddam obvious!—and now you're livin' up here too, in this city, which is one big wide dirty filthy garbage can of mixed-breeds and gypsies with no pure blood anywhere in sight. You know, I even saw a couple of nigger nuns today, and yesterday I saw a nigger priest. Wait 'til I get back down home. I'm gonna tell them about how my grannie was right from the very beginnin'. My grannie, she used to always say that the reason those Irish are priests and nuns a lot was because they have to wear all those robes and cover themselves up because the parts of their bodies that you don't see are really black! You want some proof about that? I'll give you some proof! The name Fitzgerald. It's supposed to be *Irish* . . . but you explain to me then: Ella *Fitzgerald*. And what about John—FITZGERALD —Kennedy? Hell, none of those Kennedys are pure white. We all knew that down there as soon as we found out he was really a nigger-lover! (*He takes a long slug*

of the cognac) Birds of a feather flock together! AND
YOU TWO DON'T KNOW A THING ABOUT THAT,
DO YOU? Birds of a feather flock together! When I
was in the Armed Services for our country, stationed over
in that dirty France, well, I was in charge of the arms
room—you know—the weapons. I took care of all the
M1's and all the carbines. They knew it was the right job
for me. I was given an expert rating . . . and I ain't
never been without a rifle durin' my whole life. I been
huntin' since I was five years old. And so there I was in
charge of the arms room. And one day I rigged myself up
one of those makeshift silencers and I put it on one of the
carbines and then I used to look out the window of the
arms room for hours at a time, and I would sit there and
watch all of the pigeons outside, flying and perching;
and every time I saw a *black* one I would shoot it dead!
And sometimes, there would be one that wasn't pure
white like they should'uve been—sometimes there would
be one jist like you Marcey-boy—it would be white and
gray and black: a mixed-breed type! And so I would
shoot it dead too!

(*He goes near the window*)

MARCEY (*After a pause*)   Why don't you . . .

CLARENCE   Nothing! I don't want you to say a thing! Not
unless I ask you! (*He opens the window*) Nice night out
there. (*He sits on the edge of the sill, half-singing*) Birds
of a feather . . . They flock together! You know: it's
somewhere in the Bible like that . . . (*He spits out the
window*) We always have possum and 'taters down
where I come from. I was jist now thinkin' about possum
and 'taters 'cause I'm gettin' awful hungry all of a sudden. Once I went out and shot five big fat possums all
hangin' upside down on one single branch of a big tree.
Possum and 'taters is my favorite meal. I'll bet you two
ain't ever had it before. You're too busy up here mindin'

everyone's business down in the peaceful Southlands. (*He goes to the other window and opens it too*) You know why I'm openin' the windows like this? So's when I fire at you two the sounds of the gunshot will disappear outside, twelve stories high above, and hardly anyone will hear them that way. I got this neat little silencer here, but I'm being extra careful anyway. Hey, Twila! You still gotta pee, huh? Well, you jist be patient now, girl, jist be patient. (*He gives a quick glance all around the room*) Everythin's jist about ready. I got pictures of you two on film, jist so's I can show them back down there. Especially to my ole' buddy, Billy-Boy Summers. I'll tell you, I'm really gonna have to do the job now. There ain't no more of that French cognac left. I'll bet you both are wonderin' a lot of things, aren't you? Like, for instance, why I got such good taste in my drinking habits, huh? Well, about the only thing those dirty French are good for is their cognac. Shit! I got the syph when I was over there. I slept with one of those French whores. Her name was *Bicycle Jennie* . . . you know, because all of the other G.I.'s were ridin' her ass too. And so the ole' bitch gave me the syph and it was one of the worse cases on record. First they gave me two cc.'s of penicillin. It's supposed to work, but it didn't. So they had to put me on streptomycin for a long time. Now it's a different story when I think of that little blonde girl I got on Christmas Eve . . . yeahhhhh! . . . soooo different. I ain't gettin' nuthin' from her because she was brand new! You know, when I put this shirt on I am a different person. Like I put the shirt on that night before Christmas and right away I started to think of that nice blonde baby-sitter next door to my house. I jist had to go over and pay a nice little friendly call! (*He begins to rub the hair on his chest; he fondles at his crotch*) Twila-girl, I'll bet you got a nice little pair of sweet-tastin' chocolate cupcakes, haven't you? Take off your dress, girl! G'WAN,

TAKE IT OFF! (TWILA *does not move.* MARCEY *gets up*)
Sit down, Marcey-boy! (*He laughs*) You know, my
daddy caught me in a carriage once down in our cellar
when I was only four years old. I was layin' on top of
this little girl who was about the same age as me, and you
know, my daddy was real proud of his son—Georgie Ross
Jordan! HA! HA! HA! (CLARENCE *walks away from the
window*) I'm a self-educated boy! I can do many things
. . . like, for instance, I am a good faker, don't you both
agree? I mean you two know now how I ain't the same
person that I was down in that barroom, don't you?

MARCEY (*Quickly*)   Let her go! Will you, man?

CLARENCE   Shut up!

TWILA (*Quickly*)   Let us go! Let Marcey go!

CLARENCE   Shut up!

MARCEY   You won't get away with this.
    (CLARENCE *fires once. He hits* MARCEY *in the heart.*
    MARCEY *falls over and dies.* TWILA *lets out a piercing
    scream. She becomes hysterical. She tries to run to
    MARCEY's figure on the floor, but CLARENCE pushes
    her onto the bed. She begins to fight him. He slaps
    her hard across the face. She begins to sob*)

CLARENCE   You forget about him! He ain't no longer with
us. I told him to keep his mouth shut! Besides, nigger
girl . . . the battle . . . the *real* battle . . . is between
you and *me* . . . regardless, black honey, what everyone else says!
    (*He goes and turns off the lights.* TWILA *lies sobbing
    on the bed*)

TWILA   No . . . no . . . nooooo . . .

CLARENCE   I gotta get myself a little ass first . . . ain't
that right, Miss Twila?

TWILA Please . . . don't . . . (CLARENCE *begins to take
off his pants*) NO!

CLARENCE Jist as soon as I finish layin' you, honey, it will
be all over for you. Nuthin' for you to ever worry about
again after that . . .
  (TWILA *sits up on the bed*)

TWILA Please . . . !
  (*The red and green neon sign flashes on and off
through the windows*)

CLARENCE (*Singing softly*) "The redder the rose . . .
The greener the grass . . . The blacker the nigger . . .
The sweeter the ass." (*He laughs wildly. Then he begins
to walk toward the bed.* TWILA *is motionless. He ap-
proaches her*) Don't be too scared. Don't be too nervous.
Hell, you look like a corpse, honey. You better start
smilin'. I ain't got all my clothes off yet. I'll take my shorts
off . . . but I'll leave my shirt on. This shirt makes me
do things I otherwise can't do ordinarily. I'll leave my
shirt on . . . and that way I'll show you the best time
you'll ever have in your whole life . . . before you die,
honey.
  (*He fusses with the hair on his chest*)

Blackout

Times Square

TIMES SQUARE *was first presented by the LaMama Troupe on June 4, 1967, at Experimenta II, Frankfurt, Germany, with the following cast:*

(*In order of appearance*)

BUTCH FLAGSTONE	Jerry Cunliffe
DALLAS CARNEGIE	Beth Porter
STEPHEN BEAMS	John Bakos
LAURA JEAN LINCOLN	Claris Erickson
MR. FASCINATION	Kevin O'Connor
BOBO SOCIETY	Marilyn Roberts
MARIGOLD SOBBING	Mari-Claire Charba

Directed by Tom O'Horgan

THE PEOPLE OF THE PLAY

(They are all under 25)

BUTCH FLAGSTONE, wears a bright red shirt, a radiant yellow necktie, a thick shiny belt with a brass buckle, tight white pants, and a pair of gleaming black leather boots.

DALLAS CARNEGIE, a topless waitress who wears a deep, rich red tassel dangling from each of her full and naked breasts. Below all of this she wears a pair of green satin skin-fitting lounging trousers designed for a lady. Her hair is dark and long.

STEPHEN BEAMS, dressed in faded blue denims, a striped, white and blue dress shirt with the sleeves rolled up, and purple sneakers with thick yellow bottoms.

LAURA JEAN LINCOLN, all dressed up in a clean, dainty, lemon-colored summer dress, short white gloves and white high heels. She wears a white bandana in her chestnut hair.

MR. FASCINATION, dressed in a well-tailored dress suit of luminous neon green, a fancy gold vest, a crisp white shirt, a very wide red satin necktie, and red satin-covered shoes to match.

BOBO SOCIETY, dressed to be the perfect specimen of the young modish lady of today.

MARIGOLD SOBBING, dressed in an all-white mod wedding ensemble.

WHERE THEY ARE

The celebrated block on West Forty-second Street between Broadway and Eighth Avenue in Manhattan.

WHEN

The middle of a modern summer during a twenty-four-hour period beginning at noontime.

NOTE:

The seven people of this play speak and behave and react as though they were children: playing youngish games, feeling, dreaming, wishing, quarreling, teasing, laughing, crying, and never weary . . . but sometimes, somehow, woefully uncertain.

There is no curtain. The performing areas are mainly the stage itself and sometimes various parts of the whole theatre, including the ceiling.

The stage is bare at first. The lighting is that of the bright golden sun at exactly twelve o'clock noon. We hear bells tolling the time—numerous sorts of bells. There are sounds of heavy traffic, different kinds of blaring music all at the same time; then a lone siren almost drowns it all out. BUTCH FLAGSTONE *appears onstage. He looks directly out at the audience.*

BUTCH   At the Rialto they're having the first New York showing—"A Hot Summer Game." It's a movie about the daring games of love. Over at the Times Square House of Flicks they always show two thrilling action hits: "A Man Without Morals" plus "A Girl Without Shame." They got good hot, buttered popcorn too, and it's a nice place to relax if you really aren't up to hustling your ass!

(BUTCH *smiles out at* DALLAS CARNEGIE. *She is passing out movie theatre tickets to members of the audience. There is the sound of blaring trumpets as a large, gaudy-colored backdrop slowly unfolds onstage behind* BUTCH. *He sits down on a small folding beach chair that he has brought with him. The backdrop says:* COOPED UP? FEELIN' LOW? ENJOY A MOVIE TODAY. *Below the printing there is a picture of a sadlooking man: simple-faced, round and pale, shedding tears behind prison bars. Then, more printing:*

42nd Street: The World's Greatest Movie Center. STEPHEN BEAMS *appears from the back of the theatre*)

STEPHEN   Relax! Live longer! See a movie now!

DALLAS   Why not?
(STEPHEN *begins to walk in and out of the audience as he heads toward the stage. He is covered both front and back with full-sign posters. The front poster says:* "The Mad Monk": The Most Inhuman and Unhuman Creatures Ever! To Frighten the Wits out of You!)

BUTCH (*Reading aloud*)   "The Mad Monk": The Most Inhuman and Unhuman Creatures Ever! To Frighten the Wits out of You!
(*The poster on* STEPHEN's *back reads:* Great St. Louis Bank Robbery. Steve McQueen!)

DALLAS (*Reading aloud*)   Great St. Louis Bank Robbery. Steve McQueen! Oh, good God . . . do I adore Steve McQueen!

STEPHEN   And over at the Apollo there's exhilarating excitement to be had. It's called "Web of Fear."

BUTCH   Ruthless Gunman On A Manhunt: "Minnesota Clay."

STEPHEN   Jerry Lewis. A Triple-Threat Laugh Riot! "Three On A Couch."

DALLAS   For Magnificent Summer Fun! One of the Year's Ten Best!

BUTCH   That's *me!* One of the year's ten *best!*

STEPHEN   Yeah?

BUTCH   Yeah! (BUTCH *takes out a tiny bunch of small pieces of cardboard from his pockets. He tosses them out at the audience*) Free movie tickets, everybody! They're on the house . . . free!
(*The lights come glaring up on each side of the walls of the theatre out in the audience. There is loud, uncontrolled music. On the left side of the theatre, looking at the stage, are five different signs bathed in rainbow lights:* New Amsterdam. Harris. Liberty. Empire. Anco. *On the right side of the theatre, looking at the stage, are five other signs bathed in rainbow lights:* Victory. Lyric. Times Square. Brandt's Apollo. Brandt's Selwyn)

STEPHEN   Five on one side. Five on the other side. Five and five makes ten. All open eight A.M. 'til four A.M.

BUTCH   Get More out of Life!

DALLAS   Go out to a Movie!

STEPHEN   Late Show Every Night!
(*The lights on the theatre signs in the audience begin to fade away. The sunlight on the stage begins to dim slowly*)

DALLAS   (*Going up onstage*) The weather reports are right. It's going to be a summer storm.

BUTCH   That's my luck! Shit, everybody! I gotta hustle my ass, 'cause if I don't hustle my ass, I don't eat, and if I don't eat, I don't have enough strength to hustle my ass. The rain's gonna kill everything today.
(*It gets darker*)

STEPHEN   (*Going up onstage*) Get an honest job then, man. Be legit.

BUTCH   Shit . . .

DALLAS (*To* BUTCH) He's right. Be moral.

STEPHEN I'm legit, man. I could hustle my ass. But I don't, and I won't. I get paid for carrying these signs. Not much pay. But it's okay. Enough to eat and sleep on each day. And free movie tickets; all I want. Sometimes I save money: I can sleep in the movie houses. Nothing like sleeping with the sound of cowboys having a shooting spree, Indians screaming out at me. Nothing like waking up to Ann-Margret dancing and singing at you in " 'Bye 'Bye Birdie" . . . in a bright background of bright royal blue. When you first wake up it looks like she's blowing kisses especially at you. I love Ann-Margret, I really do.

DALLAS She reminds me of a spoiled brat. She's okay, I guess, but I don't think she's too smart. I saw her once too, in person, getting off a silver jet airplane from Hollywood that flew in like a make-believe rocketship at Kennedy Airport. She's awfully short. You'd be disappointed if you saw her in the open flesh out in the open air of the outdoors with the wind blowing. Her hair was a mess. And she really *is* awfully short. *I'm* just the right height for a girl.

BUTCH If it rains today, my flesh is gonna be wasted today. (*To* DALLAS) Are you sure about the summer storm today?

DALLAS Well, can't you just tell? Look up at the sky. It's getting so dark and scary. It will probably come in a flash, and there will be terrible thunder and horrible lightning. But I'll like it a lot. Because it will make me think of my father. He would always hug me extra tight and extra long whenever there was an awful thunderstorm. (*To* BUTCH) I won't ask you to hug me when it happens. (*To* STEPHEN) I'll ask you.

BUTCH Why won't you ask me?

DALLAS   Because you don't like girls.

BUTCH   That's a lie!

STEPHEN (*To* DALLAS)   I'll be glad to hug you. But not the way your father did. I'd want to hug you the way a boy friend would want to hug you.

BUTCH (*To* DALLAS)   How can you tell that I don't like girls?

DALLAS   Well, Stephen Beams here, he recognizes my breasts. He looks at me with those two brown eyes of his, and those two brown eyes get bigger and bigger and then they begin to smile at me, his eyes do, the way two lips are supposed to smile at you . . .

STEPHEN   . . . and that's because I'm looking down at her breasts, and slowly they begin to change in my two big brown eyes, and they transform into the two most perfectly round, pure, light, pink, sugar-tasting, juicy grape-fruits . . . with a baby ripe dark cherry resting on the tip-top of each one of them!

DALLAS   Ohhhhhhh . . . that's beautiful!

BUTCH   It . . . is . . .

STEPHEN   But you, Butch Flagstone, you look down at those two sweet-tasting pieces of fruit with those extra added attractions, and what do *you* see?

BUTCH   Tell me. What, please?

STEPHEN   You see two perfectly round, perfectly shaped snowballs . . . melting away, slowly and surely disappearing, because you don't like snow . . .

BUTCH   Oh . . . I see . . .
       (BUTCH *lowers his head*)

STEPHEN   I want to hug you, Dallas Carnegie.

DALLAS   Do you really?

STEPHEN   Really and truly, Dallas Carnegie.

DALLAS   Well . . . well, we hardly know each other yet.

STEPHEN   Then let's try. Can we try?

DALLAS   I don't know yet, Stephen Beams.

BUTCH (*Lifting his head*)   The two of you are boring!

STEPHEN   What?

BUTCH   I said the two of you are boring!

STEPHEN   *You are,* man!

BUTCH   Yeah?

DALLAS   Please, both of you, don't start a fight. I hate to see boys fight each other. It isn't nice.

STEPHEN (*To* DALLAS)   I got fifty cents on me. Let's get some ice-cold beer.

DALLAS   We shouldn't get drunk.

STEPHEN   Then let's get some coffee.
(STEPHEN *takes off his signs and drops them on the floor*)

DALLAS   I love the way you look now.

STEPHEN   C'mon, let's get some coffee.

DALLAS   It's too hot for coffee. Let's have ice-cold birch beer instead.

STEPHEN   Sounds okay to me, Dallas Carnegie.

DALLAS   Then let's go, Stephen Beams.
(DALLAS *takes* STEPHEN *by the hand. There is a short pause*)

BUTCH   Not invitin' me, huh?

DALLAS   You said we were both boring.

STEPHEN   Yeah, Little Butch Flagstone! Did you forget that already?

DALLAS   But if you want to, Little Butch Flagstone, you can come with us. We'd love to have you along.

BUTCH   What else they got besides birch beer? What about real beer? They got real beer to drink there?

STEPHEN   C'mon and find out . . . Butchy-Wutchy.
(DALLAS *takes* BUTCH *by her other hand—she is in the middle now—and then the three of them leave the stage and go down through the audience. As they do it gets very dark for a moment. There is sudden thunder and lightning and then the sound of quick, fast-pouring rain. The following lines are said offstage*)

DALLAS   Hug me, hug me, hug me!

STEPHEN   Okay, Little Dallas Carnegie . . .

BUTCH   Can I . . . hug her too?

STEPHEN   Well, I don't know . . .

BUTCH   Please?

DALLAS   Of course, Little Butch Flagstone . . .

STEPHEN   Okay . . . I guess . . .

BUTCH   Thank you . . .
(*We hear the three of them laughing and giggling*

*and sighing in the dark as they disappear in the back
of the theatre. Gray sunlight emerges slowly onstage. A vague pink spotlight shines on an entranceway. Over the top it spells out in neon green letters:*
Fascination. LAURA JEAN LINCOLN *appears in the
entranceway. She is holding someone's hand through
the door. She has a marvelous Southern accent
throughout the play*)

LAURA JEAN   It's a lovely, luscious, little summer storm.
And it smells the same wherever you are—don't let them
tell you differently—be it down in Jackson or Georgia or
up here in the great big gigantic little ole' city of New
York town. Down in quiet ole' Georgia the rain, when it
falls, the warm rain down there, it waters the pretty
flowers. Up here in jumpin' Times Square town the rain,
when it falls, it waters the pretty people, the lonely people. It just simply waters the people. I think that's much
nicer, don't you, Mr. Fascination?

(MR. FASCINATION *appears. He is dressed in glowing
contrast to the sudden grayness*)

MR. FASCINATION   There's just you and me, baby. No one
else here now at Mr. Fascination's place—it's a pretty
place. Just you and me, and a little bit of new-found love
between us.

LAURA JEAN   We don't know about love yet. We just met.
It takes time.

MR. FASCINATION   I don't believe in that. It happens fast:
love. Now, c'mon, let's go. Let's find a dimly lit cocktail
lounge. I love dimly lit cocktail lounges in the summertime.

LAURA JEAN   Not in the summertime.

MR. FASCINATION   In the summertime, right here in New York City.

LAURA JEAN   Oh, no, not here in New York City.

MR. FASCINATION   In the summertime, right here in New York City. It's always been that way for me. Ever since I moved to New York City.

LAURA JEAN   But don't you think that's a sin?

MR. FASCINATION   There are only a few sins. I love dark, air-conditioned cocktail lounges on a hot stifling summer afternoon in the middle of Manhattan. I drink a fresh new rum collins every fifteen minutes. And then I begin to think. Maybe you'd say it was dreaming. I dream about falling in love. Everyone else is at the beach, and so it isn't like the way the beach should be any more. I dream about building a boat . . . a handmade raft, that's what I dream I want. A little old raft for sailing the sea. Would you like to come on my little old handmade raft with me, Miss Laura Jean Lincoln?

LAURA JEAN   You have a romantic brain.

MR. FASCINATION   I dream about falling in love.

LAURA JEAN   But you can't just dream about falling in love. You have to do more than just that.

MR. FASCINATION   But I can't fall in love, don't you see? So I must dream about it instead, see? I would like very much for you to fall in love with me. I was born under a funny star. It wasn't a very bright star. It might have been an unlucky star. And so it's twice as hard for me. It's hard to get a girl to fall in love with me. That's the way it is with some people. I'm one of them. It's tough for us. It's hard for us to trust. And the girls these days . . . well, they're so hard to please, it seems, and so that makes it even worse for me, and that's why I have all those afternoon daydreams. I wish you would fall in love with me.

LAURA JEAN   I am so confused by you.

MR. FASCINATION   That's good, then.

LAURA JEAN   It is?

MR. FASCINATION   If you're confused it's easier to fall in love, to be in love.

LAURA JEAN   It is?

(MR. FASCINATION *gives* LAURA JEAN *a light kiss on her lips.* BOBO SOCIETY *enters from the back of the theatre*)

BOBO   That's a downright precious-looking pose. Lovers on Forty-second Street. They're changing it, did you know that? I can't even think about it. I've been everywhere in the world. Mummy is rich and Daddy is dead. I've been everywhere with Mummy. I hate those other places. The people in all of those other places are hypocritical. They're dishonest. They're not to be believed. And so I've come back home . . . and now I'm visiting my favorite places . . . Forty-second Street, for instance . . . and they're changing it! I can't stand it. I just came from a movie. It was called "Sex Be My Master." It was fun. I come out and they're ripping down the Hotel Astor. (*She laughs*) How do you like that for bad modern poetry? I'll take Emily Dickinson any old day. Mummy read me Edna St. Vincent Millay. I was only five then. You can't compare them: the lovely lady American poets. I've come back home to read them again, where I belong, back home. I love home more than ever now. If the civil rights leaders want to tear down the Statue of Liberty and replace it with one of Aunt Jemima, then it's all right with me. It's perfectly justified. Besides, let's give the Statue of Liberty back to France. I've been there. A year in Paris. De Gaulle is just as bad as the Governor of Alabama. (*By now she has reached the stage*) My name is Bobo Society. (*She recites*) "My candle burns at both ends, it will not last the night. But ah, my foes . . . and oh, my friends, it gives a lovely light!" I knew that poem when I was six years old on Sutton Place South and Daddy was away in Europe being insulted and cheated and betrayed because he was an American. Have the two of you eaten dinner yet? It's exactly six o'clock now. (*The bells everywhere toll the precise time*) It's stopped raining and everything smells nice and fresh. Could I treat the two of you to dinner?

MR. FASCINATION   I would like a drink first. An ice-cold frosted rum collins in a gigantic frosted glass, two feet high.

BOBO   Then let's go.
(LAURA JEAN *takes* MR. FASCINATION'*s hand*)

BOBO (*To* LAURA JEAN)   Would it be all right if I took his other hand? I mean, you wouldn't mind, would you? I would feel much better.

LAURA JEAN   Then please do it. I wouldn't mind.

BOBO   Thank you.
(MR. FASCINATION *is now between the two girls, everyone hand in hand, as they are ready to leave the stage and go down through the audience. It is getting a bit darker now. There are the beginning signs of the lights being turned on in Times Square. We hear the offstage voices of* BUTCH, DALLAS, *and* STEPHEN *coming from the back of the theatre*)

DALLAS   Oh, God! Why are they changing it?

STEPHEN Can't even get a glass of old-fashioned birch beer any more.

BUTCH I would have loved trying that birch beer. I never had birch beer before.
(*The three of them appear in the audience, facing* LAURA JEAN, MR. FASCINATION, *and* BOBO *onstage*)

BOBO It's a goddam shame, what they're doing!

BUTCH Ruining everything!

DALLAS Let's all go out to dinner and forget all about it.

BOBO I'll buy dinner for all of us.

STEPHEN We'll eat our problems away.

MR. FASCINATION We'll drink our cares away.

LAURA JEAN We'll have hundreds of drinks made with rum.

MR. FASCINATION Leave the fags and the prostitutes and narcotic addicts alone. Let them stay here, I say! Push them out of here and where do you think they'll go? They'll go somewhere else, that's what. They have to go somewhere else. There has to be a place for them. Not imprisoned either. Outside, I say, where they can be free . . . right here on this block, what's wrong with that?
(*By now the six of them have joined hands on the stage. They dance like children to a jazzed-up version of an old familiar child's tune*)

DALLAS No one seems to appreciate me here. Maybe I should go to Europe.

MR. FASCINATION Fuck Europe!

BOBO   I agree!

STEPHEN   Let's all go and build a boat together. And then we'll all sail off together.

BUTCH   I might have better luck in another country. Maybe in England. Or France. Or Italy. Or Germany. They might respect me more there. I might make more money. I'll hustle my ass all over the face of Europe.

MR. FASCINATION   Forget it. You're better off here. I know. I've been to Europe.

LAURA JEAN   Leave the dirty bookstores alone. They're not dirty. It's all those dirty minds who think they're dirty.

MR. FASCINATION   Clean-ups! Clean-ups! Hell, clean-ups come and clean-ups go! Leave the garden alone. I mean, just look up there, everybody. Look what they did to the beautiful old Times Building. It looks like an iceberg now. I feel like I'm going to cry.

LAURA JEAN   So do I.

BOBO   Me too.

STEPHEN   I got a lump in my throat.

BUTCH   Maybe it would be a good idea if we all started crying, together.

MR. FASCINATION   They'll lock us up. They wouldn't understand.
   (*They all begin to pantomime eating, and then drinking. They are getting high on drinking. The sky is getting darker, but the lights are bright and flashing now from all the neon signs. Music is heard everywhere. They are all dancing everywhere. As*

they dance, MR. FASCINATION *goes through a verbal chant*)

BOBO   Let's find a place and hide . . . all together . . . where we can all play house together!

MR. FASCINATION (*He chants*)   If you stand . . . at the garbage can . . . blue and orange . . . garbage can . . . of course high . . . on jazzed rum . . . modern jazzed juice . . . you will see . . . a dream scene . . . from the Thirteenth Street stairway down . . . on the dream scene subway station way down . . . a scene from a rainbow dream . . . poles of black and white fourteen . . . black on white fourteen . . . black and white poles that are square . . . up we go . . . that are square and pregnant . . . they add up to forty-two . . . that are square and pregnant . . . pregnant with gum machines . . . orange waste pockets . . . like shovel chins . . . penny-chocolate machines . . . with thin orange chins . . . and baby blue Kleenex babies . . . and green baby gummers . . . with no chins at all . . . and forlorn peanut globes . . . all expecting with shining glass bellies . . . on all those quiet papa poles . . . with the proud numbers . . . from forty-two down to fourteen. (*He shouts*) Then lean! Lean among the forty-two's and fourteen's! Lean! On the army tank! Lean! On the half-an-army-tank-garbage-can! Lean!

BOBO   What's he talking about it?
        (*By now they have all worked themselves up into a frenzy*)

MR. FASCINATION (*Shouts*)   Lean! Lean! Lean!

LAURA JEAN   I'm so drunk!

ALL (*They scream*)   I'm so drunk! I'm so drunk! I'm so drunk!

BOBO   It's almost midnight now . . .

DALLAS   All the bells will be ringing soon.

LAURA JEAN   Let's play jacks.

BOBO   Jacks?

DALLAS   Let's play spin the bottle.

BUTCH   Post office! What about playing post office!

MR. FASCINATION   People used to tell me about playing spin the bottle and post office and jacks . . .

BOBO   And war and old maid and fish . . .

DALLAS   All those card games for little kids that my great big sister used to tell me all about . . .

BUTCH   Change the image, they're saying! Change the image of Times Square and Forty-second Street and everywhere else you go these days . . .

STEPHEN   These stupid changing days . . .

MR. FASCINATION   . . . and nights!
    (*The lights get brighter. We hear a zooming siren. We hear horns honking, then louder music. But finally the noise is all nearly drowned out because bells from everywhere begin to toll midnight*)

LAURA JEAN   It's twelve o'clock midnight. It's the beginning of a new day.

DALLAS   What? What did you say? I can't hear anything or anybody!

MR. FASCINATION   (*Shouting*)   What is it, anyway? Is it New Year's Eve during the middle of the afternoon during the middle of the summertime?

(There is sudden dead silence. We hear a sweet melodious voice humming from above, from the center of the ceiling over the middle of the audience)

MARIGOLD   My name is Marigold . . .
(They all look up. A long golden ladder made of thick twine comes unfolding down and then dangles about half a foot from the floor. The tolling bells are heard again, but this time they are wedding bells. We hear organ music to "Here Comes The Bride")

BOBO *(Happily)*   She's a bride!

LAURA JEAN   Such a beautiful-looking bride!

DALLAS   Like out of a fairy tale!

BUTCH   She's really pretty all in white like that!

STEPHEN   She doesn't look like she belongs here!

MARIGOLD   My name is Marigold . . .
(MARIGOLD begins to climb slowly, carefully down the ladder)

MR. FASCINATION   But . . . she's losing her smile. Hey, beautiful lady, all dressed up in your modish white bridal clothes: keep your original smile, will you?

MARIGOLD *(Sadly)*   My name is Marigold Sobbing . . .

MR. FASCINATION   But please keep your original smile . . .

BOBO   Please . . .

LAURA JEAN   Please . . .

DALLAS   Please . . .

MR. FASCINATION   She's beginning to cry. Jesus Christ, why did you have to start crying like that, Miss Marigold, why?

(*When* MARIGOLD *reaches the bottom of the ladder the three men go to assist her. She is crying soft and long now.* BOBO, LAURA JEAN, *and* DALLAS *have tears in their eyes. The wedding music turns into a very wild, crazy version of "Here Comes The Bride." The seven of them all freeze in their positions; then all of the lights go out, everywhere, and the theatre is in sudden pitch blackness*)

MARIGOLD (*In the darkness*) My name is Marigold, my name is Marigold, my name is Marigold . . . (*Her line turns from the sad crying into a lilting happy announcement*) My name is Marigold, my name is Marigold, my name is Marigold . . . (*The* Fascination *sign comes back on, blinking and flashing onstage. Music is heard again: a new sort of jazzy, wedding party music. The lights begin to come up again.* MARIGOLD *is standing in the center of the audience. The six of them have situated themselves in a staggered circle around her, relaxed and smiling in the audience*) I just flew back from everywhere. I've been to China and Japan and Russia. I was in Australia and South America and Canada. I saw Spain and France and Italy and Germany and England and Scotland and Ireland too. I went to Greece and then up to Scandanavia and then all the way back down to Istanbul. I just flew back from everywhere. My airplane was supposed to land on the top of a brand-new giant skyscraper: the Pan-Am Building in the middle of the city. I was so excited. But something went wrong, mechanically wrong up there in the cool summer air, way up there where I almost could look down and see everywhere. The plane, my airplane, stopped up there in midair above the roof of the Pan-Am Building. It was a sudden emergency. The pilot of my airplane—he looked a lot like Prince Charming—well, this handsome-looking captain of my airplane, he told us not to panic. We all

stood up. I was the closest to the button. He said to me
—The Captain Prince Charming—he told me in his deep,
smooth masculine voice that I should press the button,
the golden button, at once, immediately. But everyone
got scared. They got panic-stricken anyway. They all
rushed at me toward the gleaming golden button on the
side of the wall where I was standing. We were all in one
bunch now. None of us could move now. We were like a
bunch of frightened sardines way up there in that huge
silver sardine can that had so much room everywhere else
now. It was terrible. And now Captain Prince Charming
was really worried. None of us in the sardines' corner of
that mechanically exhausted airplane could lift our arms
nor our hands. None of us were capable of pressing that
gleaming golden button in order to save our lives. I
turned my face away from all of them, and from Captain
Prince Charming, who I was beginning to fall in love
with, and guess what happened?

BOBO   What?

LAURA JEAN   What?

DALLAS   What?

MR. FASCINATION   Go on, Miss Marigold, tell us.

MARIGOLD   My lips were facing the button. My two trembling lips were face-to-face with that gleaming golden
button that could save all of our lives . . .

STEPHEN   So what did you do?

MARIGOLD   I didn't know what to do. The button was so
golden that it almost blinded me. I turned my face away
from it and I was looking at Captain Prince Charming . . .

BOBO   Was he looking at you?

MARIGOLD   Oh, yes.

LAURA JEAN   That's really romantic.

MARIGOLD   Oh, yes.

DALLAS   It reminds me of Snow White.

BUTCH   Marigold *is* Snow White!

MARIGOLD   Oh, thank you.

MR. FASCINATION   And then what happened, Miss Marigold? C'mon, tell us.

MARIGOLD   Well . . .

STEPHEN   The suspense is killing us!

MARIGOLD   Well, Captain Prince Charming looked at me with those deep brown eyes of his and then he said to me: "Kiss it." So gently and with such tenderness and in such a soft whispering tone of voice: "Kiss it . . . Miss Marigold Sobbing . . . just simply kiss it." And so I turned away from him, and all the other passengers pushed in harder at me, and so I kissed it, the gleaming golden button that faced my two lips. I simply kissed it, and then a panel began to open underneath me before my feet and a long golden ladder made of long strong golden threads went tumbling out into the bright blue sky and unfolded in the golden-yellow specks of the sunshine all the way down, far far down, until it finally reached the earth, until it was finally down on the safe and welcome sidewalk.

MR. FASCINATION   And here you are!

MARIGOLD   I'm so happy to be back. You have no idea how happy I am to be back home. I love home. There's absolutely no place like home.

(Music comes blaring on. They all begin to dance: "the dance of the day." MARIGOLD *dances with* MR. FASCINATION, *and then he dances with* LAURA JEAN; *then back with* MARIGOLD, *etc.* STEPHEN *dances with* DALLAS; BUTCH *dances with* BOBO. *The following happens while they all dance)*

BUTCH   It's getting late. My mother hasn't called me yet. I like the snow, Stephen, I do. I like the snow, everybody. I love to eat the snow. It melts in your mouth the way sugar melts in your mouth, and you can never get acne on your face when you eat snow. In fact, everybody, it kills the acne: the eating of the sugar snow. I love to make snowballs and snowmen and snowhouses and snowcaves and igloos. I like the snow when it freezes on the gingerbread houses. And I love the pretty little girls in their pretty little snowsuits and their snowbonnets and their snowshoes. I really love them, I really do! I had a very pretty little girl friend once, and she was made of pure sugar from head to foot, pure delicious candy sugar and her very pretty face—which was really very pretty beautiful—it was an extra-special face because no one had ever kissed it before. Not a soul. And so, one day full of icicles and sweet Popsicles right before suppertime in the middle of an evergreen Popsicle playground and during the very middle of a beautiful white winter snowstorm on our way home from ice-skating together: *I kissed her* . . . on that face that had never been kissed before. And what do you think happened? *She got pregnant.* Two days later, right at twelve o'clock noon, she had a little baby, my little boy, and he was also made of pure white sugar, pure sweet delicious sugar, and he tasted even better than she did . . . there was nothing I could do about it, everybody . . . it was too late, in a way, everybody . . . he tasted even better than she did to me . . . he was made of even sweeter sugar . . .

(BUTCH *leaves them and goes onstage. He dances by himself now: he is facing the audience*)

BOBO   It's getting later and later. It reminds me of my pretty plastic white toothbrush with the pretty plastic pink rosebuds on the smooth-feeling handle . . . tonight —it's getting awfully late, everybody—tonight reminds me of my favorite toothbrush, and of my bright white teeth that never stop growing. I sold my teeth once. I sold them to a very poor old lady and a very poor old man so that they both could buy a birthday cake. They never had a birthday cake before and so that's why I sold them my teeth. I charged them . . . *nothing!* That's right, everybody: for absolutely nothing. I sold them my teeth—made so bright and clean by my own personal toothbrush, very rare—I sold them my sparkling set of lovely white teeth for *free* so that they could buy a pure whipped-cream birthday cake that was delivered down to them from the tip-top of an ancient ivory tower that was located directly in the center of a deep blue lake that was filled to its sparkling surface with hundreds of thousands of smooth ivory fish who were all the same lovely shade of white as my set of diamond teeth which I sold for free to the poor old man and the poor old lady . . .

(BOBO *begins to take down the signs on the left side of the theatre*)

STEPHEN (*Dancing*)   Go, Dallas Carnegie, go!

DALLAS (*Dancing*)   I am, Stephen Beams! *I am! I am going!* I'm going, I'm flying to the white shining moon, the white romantic moon. I'm going to float all the way up to the handsome man in the moon in the beautiful, jet-black sky, such a breathtaking jet-black, pitch-black, pure-black, smooth ebony sky. He's the man for me: the man in the moon! I love him. What's your name—I mean, your real name—Stephen Beams?

STEPHEN (*Dancing*)   My real name is The Man In The Moon!

DALLAS (*Dancing*)   I knew that was your real name.

STEPHEN (*Dancing*)   It's getting later. It'll be the beginning of daylight soon. The ebony black will turn to the ivory white and we'll be married then.

DALLAS (*Dancing*)   What shall I wear at the wedding?

STEPHEN (*Dancing*)   Your breasts. Wear your two magnificent breasts. With white tassels, that's all.

DALLAS (*Dancing*)   What a wedding it will be! And forever! I want it to last forever. Not like being young, that's not forever, being young. I wish it were forever. And so we'll make the wedding last forever. Let me kiss you. (*She does so*) Ah, hot lips, you're burning my heart and it's beginning to melt all over everybody. You'd better build a raft. We'll all cool off on your raft. We'll float on the Hudson and we'll float out to sea and we'll float on the top of the ocean around the whole country. Stephen Beams, my man in the moon, kiss me!

(STEPHEN *kisses her. The bells begin to toll. It is daylight now. The bells toll six o'clock in the morning. The music stops. They all begin to remove the theatre signs from out in the audience, assisting* BOBO. *They begin to pile the signs on the stage.* MR. FASCINATION *begins to take the backdrop down and then* STEPHEN *helps him fold it and drop it on top of the pile of signs.* MARIGOLD *falls asleep on the pile*)

MR. FASCINATION   Miss Marigold is tired. Sound asleep, just like that, in a flash! Glad to be back home. Where there are no enemies: back home. Where she won't be cheated and where she won't be conned: back here at home. I love Miss Marigold.

LAURA JEAN   But what about me, Mr. Fascination?

MR. FASCINATION   I love you too.

LAURA JEAN   But you can't have both. You can't have everything. It's me or it's her. Now tell me: who is it?

MR. FASCINATION   I don't know yet. I don't know.

BUTCH   I don't know what to do.

MR. FASCINATION   It'll be noontime soon.

LAURA JEAN   Kiss me, Mr. Fascination.

DALLAS   Let's play spin the bottle, everybody!

LAURA JEAN   Please, kiss me, Mr. Fascination.

DALLAS   Don't you want to play spin the bottle, Stephen Beams?

LAURA JEAN   I want you to kiss me, Mr. Fascination. If you kiss me then you'll be in love with me. That's what you want . . . I know that's what you want: to be in love. You told me before how you wanted to be in love. So be in love with me. We'll get married and have seventeen children. Boys and girls. And then you know what we'll do? We'll give them syrup. A special kind of syrup. We'll make the syrup together, you and I, Mr. Fascination. We'll make the syrup together. In bed, together. The sweetest-tasting syrup imaginable. We'll only make the syrup while we're in our wedding bed together. It will always be called "The Wedding Bed." "Our Wedding Bed." We'll call it by that name even when we're one hundred years old and all of our seventeen children are still six years old. We'll make the syrup by kissing, in our bed, our wedding bed . . . we'll wish together— the same wish, our own secret wish—and then we'll kiss. We'll wish our wish and kiss our kiss: and that's how the syrup will be made. We'll keep a crystal vase near our pink and blue pillows, and after we wish and then after we kiss, we'll lower our faces to the very brim, the very delicate edge of the crystal vase, and then we'll let the syrup flow from our eyes into the gentle crystal vase. And every Christmas and every Easter and every other holiday known to man, we'll feed the syrup to our seventeen children, and they will remain children forever. Their imaginations will be in full bloom forever . . . and they will never die. Everything will be forever . . .

(MR. FASCINATION *kisses* LAURA JEAN *for a long time*)

DALLAS   Let's play jacks. Let's play anything. I love to play. I love to play nice, innocent games. If we can't play spin the bottle because we don't have a bottle, then let's play any old game. I don't care. Let's play "what you're thinking and what I'm thinking." That's a good game. But I still would rather play spin the bottle first. It's a human game. I love good innocent human games most of all.

BUTCH   I found one! I found one! I found a bottle! An empty milk bottle for spin the bottle!

DALLAS   Oh, that's perfect! And an empty *milk* bottle! That makes it even more perfect—if it's a *milk* bottle!
(BUTCH, LAURA JEAN, DALLAS, *and* BOBO *all sit down in a circle in the center of the audience underneath the golden ladder.* MARIGOLD *begins to wake.* MR. FASCINATION *goes to her*)

MR. FASCINATION   Would you like to play a game with all of us? Would you like to play spin the bottle?

MARIGOLD   I had such a lovely dream . . .
      (STEPHEN *is the last to join the circle. He stands in
      the center of it*)

STEPHEN   Miss Marigold Sobbing. Please do join us, Miss
Marigold Sobbing. We're all about to have fun. Lots and
lots of fun-fun.

MARIGOLD   I love to have fun.

MR. FASCINATION   We all love to have fun.

DALLAS   Spin the bottle is the best fun of all. We'll all sit
here in this nice cozy friendly circle, see?

MARIGOLD   I see . .

STEPHEN   And we'll all pretend we're sitting down beneath
a lilac tree, see. A sweet-smelling purple-lavender lilac
tree: a great billowing bush full of blue buds and soft
summer leaves. We'll sit in the grass and it will scratch us
a little, at first it will scratch us when we sit, and it will
be good scratching because it will make us all feel so relaxed. We'll all be free and easy and ready for kissing.
It's the most important thing known to man: kissing.
Just plain good old-fashioned kissing . . . and sometimes just plain good old-fashioned soul-kissing. This is
it, girls and boys! The last lilac tree in the world. We've
got to keep it alive. We can't let the last lilac die. The last
lilac tree, and it's right here, of all places, in the middle
of Forty-second Street. Now, c'mon, Miss Marigold Sobbing, come and play our game with us.

BOBO   Please?

DALLAS   Pretty please?

LAURA JEAN   Pretty pretty please?
      (MARIGOLD *begins to get up off the pile of signs and
      posters;* MR. FASCINATION *helps her.* MARIGOLD *stands*

on the stage and looks out at them all. STEPHEN *sits
down and joins the circle.* MR. FASCINATION *stands
holding* MARIGOLD's *hand*)

MARIGOLD   Lilac trees are my favorite trees. Cotton candy
is my favorite candy. Doves are my favorite birds. Raspberry sherbert is my favorite ice cream. Kissing means
love. And I love kissing. And so love is my favorite pastime. And believing what you dream . . . what you imagine! Well, now, that's the most favorite, the truest pastime of them all.

  (MR. FASCINATION *begins to lead* MARIGOLD *off the
  stage. When they reach the stairs and are ready to
  go down into the audience, a series of loud blasting
  gunshots is heard.* MARIGOLD *screams. All of the girls
  scream. The men freeze.* MARIGOLD *drops into* MR.
  FASCINATION's *arms. There is a dead silence*)

MR. FASCINATION   (*Finally*)   Miss Marigold! Miss Marigold! Miss Marigold Sobbing!
  (*A siren is heard in the distance*)

DALLAS   (*Hysterically*)   Someone's in trouble! Whenever
you hear a siren it means someone's in trouble! My
mother always told me that! And so I would cry because
I didn't want anyone to ever be in trouble if they didn't
deserve to be in trouble! (*Getting up*) Look at her! Miss
Marigold Sobbing! She's in trouble! Can't you all see that
she is in terrible horrible trouble?

STEPHEN   Sit back down, Dallas!

BUTCH   There's nothing we can do about it, Dallas.

DALLAS   (*Sitting back down*)   But she's in awful trouble.
  (*She begins to sob. The siren gets closer*)

LAURA JEAN (*Sobbing*)   I don't understand why she has to be in trouble. It's not right. If we're not in trouble then why should Miss Marigold Sobbing be in trouble?

BOBO (*Sobbing*)   There must be something we can do about it. We can't just sit here and ignore it. We can't just sit here and go ahead with our game.
(*The siren builds into a blasting scream and then stops.* MR. FASCINATION *lies* MARIGOLD *gently down on the floor of the stage*)

MR. FASCINATION   Go ahead, you kids.

DALLAS   But we can't.

MR. FASCINATION (*Sternly*)   I said to go ahead with your game, you kids!

STEPHEN   We forgot how to play it.

BUTCH   I never knew how to play it.

MR. FASCINATION   Then I'll tell you how to play it. First of all . . .

DALLAS   Is she dead?

MR. FASCINATION   I said I'll tell you how to play it! First of all now . . .

BOBO   Just tell us if she's dead or not, that's all . . .

LAURA JEAN   . . . and then we'll go ahead and play it.

MR. FASCINATION (*He speaks into a bullhorn*)   I said that I would tell you how to play it! First of all now, each of you get back down into the circle, underneath the world's last lilac tree, the last billowing bush of its kind on earth. Now, you've got the bottle. You're sitting on the fresh-smelling grass, see. It tickles a little at first—it doesn't scratch—it tickles, remember that, and it feels so nice, and it makes you all feel so relaxed. Forget about all the changes . . . everywhere. Remember that great huge photograph up the street in the great huge empty window that used to be the Crossroad's Café? I know you all saw that photograph today. It has a picture of what they're going to do to this block someday very soon now. They're going to turn it into a plaza, see? It's going to look like all of the millions of new plazas that are going up everywhere, every day, all over the country, see? The same kinds of plazas that the Europeans are putting up all over Europe, see? I know, I know, I know! It all looks like a graveyard with lots of fake green trees! Well, forget it! I'm going to teach you how to play spin the bottle again. This is what you do. It's someone's turn to spin the bottle in the middle of the circle. If a boy spins the bottle it has to point to a girl. If it points to the girl then he gets to kiss her. He has to keep spinning the bottle until it points to a girl. After he kisses her then it's her turn to spin the bottle. When she does it has to point to a boy. She keeps spinning it until it points to a boy. Then she kisses him. And now it's his turn to spin the bottle. You see? It's all very simple. Now, g'wan. Play the game like you all started out to do in the first place.

BUTCH Who should do it first?

MR. FASCINATION Since you asked first, *you* do it first, Butch Flagstone. (*Reluctantly, they begin to play the game. Slowly they get into it until eventually they are all enjoying it. The game goes on until almost the end of the play. The five of them seem hypnotized in the playing of it, and the game works up into a steady and final type of children's celebration. During the entire game* MR. FASCINATION *speaks into the bullhorn. The five of them don't really hear what he has to say*) It will be high noon soon.

I'd like to go somewhere maybe and build a small boat.
(*To* MARIGOLD) Why did you have to go and get killed
like that? *Why?* (*Softly*) I'm sorry. I guess I need a drink.
A tall rum collins in an air-conditioned cocktail lounge.
I would go there and I would pretend that I was going to
meet someone like you there, Miss Marigold Sobbing.
And I would kiss you when you weren't looking and
then I would fall in love with you. (*He sighs*) I feel as
though I'm getting sick. Hey! Hey, now wait a minute!
Wait just one minute! (*He wipes his eyes*) I think I'm
seeing things. (*He rubs his eyes*) I'm seeing things! I
see a bunch of peppermint sticks. A small group of peppermint sticks, red and white peppermint sticks with
tiny little smiling faces on them. One, two, three, four,
five, six, seven. There are seven of them. Gee, they really
look great, all seven of them! Oh, wait a minute now.
There's a whole bunch of other peppermint sticks in the
picture all of a sudden. They don't have any color to
them. They're just plain-looking peppermint sticks. Jesus
Christ, there are hundreds of them . . . thousands of
them . . . coming from everywhere. (*He screams*) Hey!
You stop that! (*He begins to giggle*) Hey, c'mon, now!
You stop that, will you! (*He is giggling louder and
longer*) Ohhhhhhhhhhh! You gotta stop that! Hey, you'll
drive the seven of us out of our minds! (*Laughing*) We'll
all die . . . laughing! And that's no fooling! Now, c'mon,
you people, stop it! Stop sucking at us like that! Stop that
licking, will you? I'll cut off your selfish tongues! The
seven of us will! We'll start fighting all of you . . . we'll
cut off your tongues every which way . . . if you don't
stop *sucking* at us like that! (*He is laughing again*)
You're going to drive us out of our minds. You're going
to suck all of the color and all of the sugar out of our
systems. (*Suddenly violent*) Can't you hear me? (*He
half-laughs, half-screams*) And leave her alone! She's not
as strong as the rest of us. She's sweeter and richer but

she's not as strong, because everyone wants to suck at her, lick her dry with their selfish murderous wild tongues! (*Shouting*) Leave her alone! You're all going to kill her! You'll suck her dry! Please don't do that. (*Moaning*) Please? She's the sweetest of all . . . the fairest of all . . . the richest of all! Will you, will you, will you sucking, licking, murdering bastards and sons-and-daughters-of-slaughtering-bitches take your filthy rotten tongues off her peppermint body? How do you stop them? What do you do? Hey! Hey! (*He screams down at the five of them*) Hey! It's Mr. Fascination! Tell me what to do! (*They all turn and look up at him*) How do you stop them? How do you bring the dead back to life? (*There is a short pause*) It's . . . almost high noon. They're ruining everything. They're changing everything around us. (*A pause*) What . . . do I do?

STEPHEN (*Finally*) Kiss her.

MR. FASCINATION What?

BOBO Kiss her.

BUTCH Kiss her.

LAURA JEAN Kiss her on the lips.

DALLAS That's all you have to do.

MR. FASCINATION What?

ALL (*They speak together*) The lips. Kiss her on the lips.

MR. FASCINATION But they're all sucking away at her lips. Octopuses! Dead white octopuses, that's what they are now. They're not even dead white peppermint sticks any more. Look at them! I can't stand it! They're taking all of the pure sweetness from her lips, all the pure color, all the deep richness. Soon there will be nothing left of her. They will tongue her to death . . . such her lips and brains and breasts . . . and her great gorgeous cunt! That eternal glorious cunt with that fountain of youth always gushing out of it! I can't let them do that! I can't stand here and allow them to suck the juices dry from that loving lilac cunt!

STEPHEN   Then kiss her!

BUTCH   Please, man!

BOBO   Kiss . . .

LAURA JEAN   Kiss . . .

DALLAS   Kiss . . .
(*They have all gathered about the foot of the stage now.* MR. FASCINATION *kisses* MARIGOLD. *She awakens. He picks her up in his arms and then begins to carry her down off the stage. The bells begin to toll noontime.* MR. FASCINATION *carries* MARIGOLD *down through the audience*)

MARIGOLD   I must have been dreaming. I dreamt I was in this airplane and it was stuck in midair above the roof of the Pan-Am Building. We were like a bunch of frightened sardines all jammed up in one corner of the airplane together. And then I saw my pilot, my captain, he was like Prince Charming, and he told me to press the gleaming golden button, and the only way I could do it was to kiss it with my lips in order to save our lives . . .
(*They all follow slowly behind* MR. FASCINATION *and* MARIGOLD)

BOBO   And then what happened?

DALLAS   Yes, do tell us!

LAURA JEAN   The suspense is killing us!

MR. FASCINATION   Well, that's what she did: she kissed it!
   (*The wedding march is heard again: a modern version. The wedding bells continue to toll. The sun is
   full-blast now. The single-file procession finally disappears into the back of the theatre*)

Blackout

About the Author

Leonard Melfi was born and educated in Binghamton, New York, and attended St. Bonaventure University, the American Academy of Dramatic Arts and the Herbert Berghof–Uta Hagen Studios.

After spending two years in Europe in the U.S. Army Mr. Melfi came to New York City determined to be an actor. Abandoning this profession, he wrote poetry for a year, had two poems published and then began to write plays. Supporting himself by taking various odd jobs, Mr. Melfi finally resorted to pawning nearly everything he owned, but continued to write. His plays have been produced at the Café LaMama, Theatre Genesis, the Playwrights Unit, Actors Studio and The Circle-in-the-Square.

Mr. Melfi was awarded a Rockefeller Foundation grant in 1967. He is a member of the Actors Studio, The Eugene O'Neill Memorial Theatre Foundation and The Playwright's Unit of Albee-Barr-Wilder. At present he lives in New York.